FRACTURED JEWEL

A Starstruck Novella

BRENDA HIATT

dolphin star
PRESS

Fractured Jewel

A Starstruck Novella

Copyright © 2016 Brenda Hiatt
Cover art by Fantasia Frog Designs

Dolphin Star Press

ISBN-13: 978-1-940618-67-8

Dedication

For my fabulous readers, who begged for more stories in this world. This one's for you!

Contents

Flawless

WITH A HAPPY SIGH, I nestled closer to Rigel in the back sea
his parents' car as they drove me home from the Jewel H
Homecoming dance and the most perfect evening of my er
life. Even being named Junior Class Princess couldn't compai
spending three whole worry-free hours with Rigel—danc
sharing loving thoughts, stealing an occasional kiss when
chaperones weren't watching…

Best of all was knowing we had a whole future to
forward to—together.

"I understand your aunt was finally told the truth this &
noon?" Rigel's dad asked, breaking into my contented thougl

"She was," I replied, "though it took Mrs. O'Gara and K
while to convince her it was all true, especially since I didn't
a chance to prepare her before the President showed up. I
really interested to see how she acts toward me—toward
us—now."

"She should at least lighten up on all the rules and chor
usually dumps on you. Right?" Rigel gave me a sideway
with the arm he had draped across my shoulders.

I smiled up at him. "Hope so." It would be especially great if she was willing to let me spend more time with Rigel.

"What was she told, exactly?" Dr. Stuart asked from the front seat. "Lili O'Gara mentioned they'd spoken but didn't give any specifics."

Understandable, since the Stuarts and O'Garas couldn't very well discuss Martian stuff while chaperoning a high school dance.

"We were already running late, so there was only time for the basics," I told her. "The colony on Mars, how I ended up on Earth, and that I'm now the Sovereign. Oh, and that I was actually on Mars over the summer instead of Ireland, and how Rigel and I sort of, um, saved the world last night."

"How did she take it?" She turned partway around to regard me curiously.

"I'm not sure," I admitted. "I think she was too boggled to say much. She's bound to have a gazillion questions now that it's had time to sink in, though."

"That may take a while," Dr. Stuart cautioned, concern furrowing her brow.

I blinked at her in surprise. "Why?"

"Such a revelation must challenge everything she thought she knew. She may need time to adjust. If that should prove to be the case, I recommend you not rush her."

I nodded, though knowing Aunt Theresa I considered it a lot more likely she'd demand every last detail before letting me go to bed tonight. For now, I was happy to just snuggle—discreetly—against Rigel for the rest of the ride home.

"What do you say we spend some time together in the arboretum tomorrow afternoon?" he murmured as he walked me to my front door a few minutes later. "Maybe get ice cream first, then spend some time just…chilling."

"Sounds perfect, especially after the week we've just had." I squeezed his arm. "It's a date."

2

Smiling, he kissed me good night. His lips on mine felt impossibly good, sending wonderful sensations sizzling through my body.

"G'night, M," he whispered. "See you tomorrow."

I was still floating on air when I turned to go inside.

"Ah, you're finally home." Aunt Theresa emerged from the kitchen as I walked in. "It's almost midnight."

"Sorry. Dr. and Mr. Stuart were chaperones at the dance, so we couldn't leave until most people were gone. We came straight here after, though, just like I promised."

Still smiling, I braced myself for the barrage of questions sure to follow. If my aunt weren't ready to talk yet, like Dr. Stuart suggested, she would have already gone to bed, to avoid me entirely.

"Hmph. Well, you'd best get to bed. It's late." She yawned, one hand over her mouth.

I blinked. Really? No questions at all? "You didn't *have* to wait up."

One gray eyebrow rose. "I always have. Why should tonight be any different?"

"I just thought… Never mind. Did you tell Uncle Louie about—?"

She gave a little twitch, her expression now shuttered. "I haven't spoken with your uncle about anything out of the ordinary this evening."

I nodded uncertainly. "That's…good, I guess." I'd been the one to suggest she not tell him. "But isn't there anything you wanted to—"

"I'd rather not stay up talking tonight, if you don't mind. As I said, it's late. Good night, Marsha."

"G'night, Aunt Theresa."

I slowly mounted the stairs, feeling slightly disoriented. Taking time to adjust was one thing, but she was acting like that conversation earlier had never even happened.

Had the Council sent someone here after I left to erase my aunt's memory or something? As soon as I reached my room, I checked my omni, since Kyna, as head of the Council, definitely would have messaged me if they had.

I needed to get in the habit of checking for messages more often anyway, since not doing so had nearly been disastrous this afternoon. What if the President had shown up while I was still in my underwear? Shuddering at the thought, I pulled the little communication device out of my nightstand drawer. No message this time.

Could Dr. Stuart be right that my aunt wasn't ready to accept the truth yet?

True, it was still hard for *me* to believe everything that had happened the past few days. First, those super-advanced aliens, the Grentl, appearing in orbit without warning. Me, Marsha Truitt, personally warning several of the leaders of the free world. Then, last night, Rigel and me surviving, against all odds, when our desperate, last-ditch effort kept the Grentl from zapping Earth back to the Stone Age.

Still, denial seemed totally out of character for Aunt Theresa. Probably she was just tired, like she'd said, so decided to wait until after church tomorrow to start pumping me for details about the whole Martian thing. I just hoped once the interrogation started, it wouldn't go on so long it delayed my date with Rigel.

But even if it did, I realized, Rigel and I now had the rest of our lives to be together! Grinning at that wonderful thought, I started to tuck my omni back into its hiding place in an old glasses case, then shrugged and left it on my nightstand. Assuming Aunt Theresa's memory *hadn't* been wiped, I didn't have to keep secrets from her any more.

Even better, now that word had gone out to all the Martians

about what Rigel and I accomplished last night, and how it was our *graell* bond that made it possible, we no longer had to worry about them constantly trying to keep us apart.

All things considered, my life should get way easier from now on. In fact, only twenty-four hours after thinking I might not have one at all, my future was looking pretty darned awesome!

———

Walking to church the next morning, it was obvious from Uncle Louie's cheerful chatter that he was still blissfully clueless about all the Martian stuff. However, the doubtful glances Aunt Theresa kept shooting my way confirmed there was nothing wrong with her memory.

She definitely remembered. She just hadn't wanted to talk about it last night.

When we reached our usual pew, the O'Garas were already there.

"I'm glad you're here," Molly told me as her mother and my aunt headed for the choir room to warm up. "I wanted to stay in bed this morning, but Mum wouldn't have it."

Brown-haired, gray-eyed and almost always bubbly, Molly had gradually become my closest friend this past year—especially since I could never tell my longtime friends Bri and Deb the truth about myself.

"There was no point even suggesting that to Aunt Theresa," I said with a laugh, "though she was yawning a little over breakfast, too, since she waited up for me."

Molly's older brother Sean—my so-called "destined Consort" according to Martian traditions—slanted a glance my way. "To ask you questions?"

"No, actually. So far she seems to be pretending yesterday's conversation never happened."

"Huh. Maybe give her time? Change can be hard, you know."

Dr. Stuart had said the same thing, but I knew Sean wasn't only talking about Aunt Theresa. He'd *seemed* to have a good time last night with his date, Homecoming Queen Missy Gillespie, but it was clear he was still struggling with the whole idea of Rigel and me being a couple again.

Sean was tall and really handsome, with thick coppery hair and bright blue eyes. But Rigel was absolute perfection—to me, anyway. And had been since the first day I'd met him.

Even as I thought that, I felt Rigel's distinctive vibe—a happy surprise, since it was the first time he and his parents had come to church since my return to Jewel four weeks ago, right before school started.

Hey! I thought to him as they headed to one of the remaining empty pews, a few rows up and to the right. *Sleep well?*

Yep. I dreamed about you…again.

Ditto. I grinned at him, then noticed Sean's frown, so started fiddling with my program. After witnessing what our *graell* bond could do last week, Sean claimed he understood now why Rigel and I had to be together but it seemed mean to flaunt it in front of him.

Rigel and I "chatted" a little more during the service, mostly about the alone time we planned for this afternoon. We still had a lot of catching up to do after three months of pretending to be apart, then three more of *really* being apart.

After the service, during the usual socializing as everyone slowly made their way toward the door, several people made a point of congratulating me on making Homecoming Court. I thanked them politely, of course, but Aunt Theresa positively beamed while responding much more effusively.

I did my best to ignore her subtle bragging, which would have made me uncomfortable even if it didn't seem so out of character. Angling away from her, I instead focused on snagging a few minutes with Rigel before we left—until another conversation caught my attention.

"—and even more arriving this week, she told me." Mrs. Billingsley, who owned Belinda's Books on Diamond Street, tapped her finger on the side of her nose. "She said the ones she saw look like they're fresh out of college."

"There was an article in the Indy Star business section this morning about it," old Mrs. Batten said. "Louise read it to me. Some high-tech GMO company moving its headquarters here."

Melinda Stevens, who waited tables at the Lighthouse Cafe, joined the group. "Four of the new folks—two couples—stopped in for dinner last night. They sounded like they're from hoity-toity schools back East but at least they're good tippers. Not real talkative, but nice enough. All of them looked like they could have been magazine models, too." She waggled her eyebrows. "Wonder if they'll be hiring locally?"

"Not so far," Mr. Strauss, the grocery store manager volunteered. "Billy was out by the old transmission plant and asked one of the workers putting up those new fences around it. Sounds like they'll be doing some kind of sensitive research, so they're bringing in all their own people. At least to start."

"Long as they spend their money locally, I won't complain," Agatha Payton declared. "They can stop by Glitterby's any old time they want, 'specially if they're that easy on the eyes," she added with a cackle.

I kept moving and reached Rigel a moment later. "Are you hearing any of this?" I asked as we clasped hands, recharging each other. "Do you think—?"

He nodded. "My dad mentioned something at breakfast about more *Echtrans* moving to Jewel. Sounded like something the Council already had in the works before…you know."

Before the Grentl showed up on Earth's doorstep a week ago.

"Some have been trickling in since late last year, but this

sounds bigger." I bit my lip. "I wonder why the Council hasn't said anything to *me* about it?"

His parents joined us then, followed by my aunt and uncle and all four O'Garas. Aunt Theresa, I noticed, spoke a lot more politely to the Stuarts and especially Rigel than she had previously. I also thought she seemed slightly nervous around both them and the O'Garas. When we got home, I'd try to reassure her that they—and I—weren't anything to be scared of.

We were nearly to the church door when Mrs. Crabtree, who lived across the street from us, accosted my aunt.

"Theresa! Do tell, *why* were those black, official-looking cars at your house yesterday? You and Louie haven't been up to anything nefarious, have you? They looked like they might be from the government or something."

Aunt Theresa froze, sending a panicked look first at me, then at Mrs. O.

"We saw those cars, too," Miss Batten chimed in from just behind us. "They drove down Diamond and turned up Opal just as Mother and I were locking up Quilt World. You said it probably had something to do with that explosion near the high school Friday night, didn't you, Mother?"

Before she could answer, Molly piped up with, "It did, actually, but it turned out to be a prank."

"A prank?" Mrs. Crabtree echoed doubtfully.

Molly nodded. "I was at M's house helping her get ready for the Homecoming dance when some men from the FBI showed up. Apparently someone called in a fake report that M knew something about that explosion. Probably a girl jealous she didn't make Homecoming court, trying to keep M from getting to the dance in time to be crowned Junior Class Princess."

Trying to hide my admiration at Molly's quick thinking, I nodded. "They acted like they already suspected it wasn't true, but they still had to check things out. They just asked me a few questions, made a quick search of our house and left. Still, it was a little scary, wasn't it Aunt Theresa?"

Still looking slightly stunned, she bobbed her head. "Er, yes. Yes, it was."

Uncle Louie looked at us both curiously. "Why didn't you—?"

"Not now, Louie," my aunt snapped. "That is, I, er, didn't want to worry you over nothing."

Mrs. O'Gara took charge then, saying something about lunch waiting and herding us all outside—probably because Aunt Theresa wasn't managing to look nonchalant at all. We said goodbye to the Stuarts and had just started walking with the O'Garas up Emerald Street when Uncle Louie said, "The FBI really came to our house yesterday?"

"Yeah, it was like Molly said, just a jealous classmate trying to cause trouble." I answered quickly so Aunt Theresa wouldn't have to lie to him.

Before Uncle Louie could ask any more questions, Mr. O changed the subject. "I understand a front is expected to come through later today and cool things down a bit. That will be a relief, won't it?"

The rest of us agreed a little too enthusiastically, but Uncle Louie didn't seem to notice anything weird about it. Not that he'd ever been particularly perceptive. We all determinedly talked about the weather until we got to our house. The O'Garas kept walking—they lived around the corner on Opal Street.

Once inside, Uncle Louie went into the living room and turned on a football game while Aunt Theresa busied herself making lunch. I joined her in the kitchen, figuring this would be a good opportunity to reassure her about everything.

"Aunt Theresa, I know you're probably a little—"

"Marsha, would you mind getting the cold cuts and cheese out of the refrigerator?" she interrupted. "Oh, and the mayonnaise as well."

After a startled moment, I complied. The sense of surrealism I'd felt so often over the past week started creeping back as she built sandwiches for all of us, meticulously placing the cheese, then the lettuce, just so.

"You weren't home to do any of your usual Saturday chores yesterday," she said after a moment, not looking at me. "Will you be able to do them today, or do you have other, er, plans?" I detected a trace of the same nervousness she'd displayed around the O'Garas and Stuarts at church.

"I promised Rigel I'd meet him in town sometime this afternoon, but I should have time to get my chores done first. Especially since it looks like Uncle Louie already mowed the lawn."

"I did that myself, before he came home from work last night. Here, set these on the table for me. Er, please."

She was being as weirdly polite to me as she'd been to the Stuarts at church but otherwise she seemed determined to act like nothing was different. And maybe, with the Grentl crisis over, everything would run smoothly enough that *her* life wouldn't need to change much at all.

I'd kind of hoped mine would, though…

2

Facets

AFTER LUNCH, Uncle Louie went back to watching football and I caught up on my Saturday chores of bathroom cleaning and vacuuming. Once that was done, I ran upstairs to brush my hair and pocket my omni before finally heading over to the arboretum —and Rigel.

He arrived at the entrance on his bike at the same time I arrived on foot. After a hello kiss—quick, but still *so* good—we walked hand in hand through the archway. The weather had clouded over since this morning and the breeze smelled like rain but there were still a surprising number of people strolling around the arboretum. There was even a couple sitting on "our" bench in the back corner, a baby in a stroller next to them.

"Kinda crowded for what I had in mind," Rigel murmured to me with that crooked smile that always made my heart speed up. "Want to go hit Dream Cream first, see if the weather chases some of these folks off later on?"

"Sure. As long as I'm with you, I'm happy."

Though I hoped we'd manage a real makeout session before I had to go home, openly holding hands with Rigel while walking down Diamond Street felt pretty darned special after being forced to hide our relationship for so long.

We'd just reached the first couple of shops in Jewel's little business district when we detected *Echtran* vibes just ahead. Scanning the Sunday afternoon shoppers on the sidewalk in front of us, I easily spotted the source—a man and two women, all noticeably more attractive than average, looking through the front window of the Gems of Jewel art gallery.

Out of habit, we paused—then I gave a little laugh. "Hey, what are we afraid of? After what we did Friday night, nobody can possibly condemn us for being together now. Right?"

"Oh. Yeah. Right." He returned my grin. "C'mon, let's make nice—and hope they don't go all gaga over you."

Since word went out last Fall that the long-lost princess (me) had been discovered alive in Jewel, a steady stream of *Echtrans* had made what were practically pilgrimages to gawk at me. Some had been so obvious I was surprised none of the locals suspected anything. I braced myself as we approached the small group.

Just as we'd sensed them, they felt our *brath* before we reached them. Three sets of eyes widened as they turned and saw me, but to my relief none of them blurted anything out. I took the initiative anyway, just to be on the safe side.

"You're all new here, aren't you? Welcome to Jewel." I smiled, trying to project an easy, casual attitude in hopes they'd mimic it.

The man stiffened for an instant, his right fist instinctively coming halfway to his chest for the traditional salute before he self-consciously dropped it to his side. The two women continued staring for another second or two, then relaxed into echoing smiles as the initial spurt of alarm I'd sensed faded into mild nervousness.

"Thank you," the older of the two women said after a barely-awkward pause. "We only just arrived last night, so haven't had as much time as some of our, ah, coworkers to settle in yet. But it seems…a lovely place. I'm Maddy."

"I'm Leila," the other woman piped up, "and this is my husband, Darby. We're honored to be among those chosen to come here and *very* pleased to meet you…er…"

"I'm sorry, I should have introduced myself right off," I said quickly, for the benefit of any Jewelites within earshot, since these three clearly knew perfectly well who I was. "I'm Marsha Truitt, and this is Rigel Stuart."

As our new acquaintances glanced quickly back and forth between Rigel and me, then down at our clasped hands, all three smiles froze. The excited nervousness I'd sensed gave way to outrage, even hostility.

"It's true then!" the man Darby whispered fiercely, now positively glaring at Rigel. "After pretending to be a hero, you completely went back on your promise to—"

"That's enough." I cut off whatever he'd been about to say, stunned by their abrupt shift in attitude. "I owe Rigel my life many times over, not to mention—"

Rigel tightened his grip on my hand, reminding me that I couldn't create a scene in the middle of Diamond Street, surrounded by *Duchas* locals. Gently, he began tugging me away.

Let it go, M. This isn't—

No! I won't go all Royal on them right now, but I won't let it go. I won't let anyone—

Really, M, it's okay. He kept tugging.

Darby had gone scarlet at my interruption. He didn't say anything else, but kept looking daggers at Rigel—as did the two women with him.

"Know that I consider disrespect toward Rigel disrespect toward *me*," I informed them, so quietly no non-*Echtran* could possibly hear me. "It won't be tolerated. Period." Then, in a normal voice, "Have a nice day."

Turning pointedly away, I continued down the street still hand in hand with Rigel. I could feel him trying to send calming thoughts my way, but it was a full minute before my irritation subsided enough for them to penetrate.

"What's *wrong* with those people?" I finally muttered, still too upset to send coherent sentences silently. "Don't they realize—?"

Maybe not. Rigel's thoughts and emotions were nowhere near as agitated as mine. *Maybe they haven't heard yet about what happened Friday night. If all they know is from that article in the* Enquirer... He shrugged.

After a few deep breaths, I managed to reply mentally. *I'm going to give that Gwendolyn Gannett a piece of my mind. She had no business printing all of Gordon Nolan's lies about you without even checking them out. I'll make her print a retraction if she doesn't do it on her own. Which she totally should.*

Seriously, it's okay, he insisted, throwing an arm around my shoulders to give me a sideways hug. *As long as nobody's trying to physically separate us, I can handle a few insults.*

I shook my head, still pissed. *It's not right. You risked your life to save all of theirs!*

So did you. Those three are probably just an isolated case, he thought soothingly as we reached Dream Cream. Then, aloud, "C'mon, I'll get you an ice cream—mint chocolate chip. That always makes you feel better."

It did. After half an hour and a hot fudge sundae with mint chip ice cream, I was much more willing to accept Rigel's explanation for the disturbing encounter we'd just experienced. He was right —it would take time for the full story of what we'd done Friday to reach everyone, especially people in the middle of moving to a new town. Shoot, they probably didn't even have their internet hooked up yet.

A light drizzle was falling when we went back outside.

"Let's head back to the arboretum," Rigel suggested. "I've got a fold-up umbrella attached to my bike."

I readily agreed, longing for that makeout session more than ever now. The rain picked up as we hurried down Diamond Street, quickly thinning the Sunday shopping crowd. By the time we reached the arboretum again, it was deserted. Just like we'd hoped.

Rigel unstrapped the umbrella from his bike's crossbar and opened it. Holding it over both of us, he threw his other arm around me and we headed to our favorite bench, out of sight from the entrance. Unfortunately, just as we reached it, a breeze kicked up, making the umbrella a lot less effective.

I squinted up at Rigel, who was trying to angle the umbrella to shield me better—and getting himself wetter in the process. On sudden impulse, I pulled out my omni. Sensing Rigel's startled alarm, I just grinned.

"Hey, nobody's here but us." I brought up its little holographic screen and a moment later our bench was dry and an invisible shield made the rain sheer away just before it touched us.

His disapproval faded into anticipation. Folding the umbrella, he sat on the bench and drew me down next to him. "I ought to be lecturing you that it's not safe to use that thing in public, but you're right—I don't see anyone joining us in this weather. Besides, I'd rather not have to juggle an umbrella right now."

He put both arms around me and for the next blissful half hour we didn't focus on anything but each other, kissing to our hearts' content and rejoicing that we'd be able to do this a lot from now on.

"Oh, good, you're home," Aunt Theresa greeted me when I got back. "Once you've washed your hands, would you mind setting the table?"

"Oh, um, sure."

I expected her to ask me *something* about where I'd been all afternoon—or at least why I wasn't wetter—but she didn't.

"Squires Electronics and Glitterby's both called, asking if you can come by late tomorrow afternoon for publicity photos with the rest of the Homecoming Court. I told them I believed you would be available?"

"I should be." I remembered Rigel doing that sort of thing after last year's Homecoming, grumbling that it was time he couldn't spend with me. Trina, last year's Sophomore Princess to his Prince, had loved it, of course.

Uncle Louie was still watching football in the living room, so I tried again to broach the subject she'd avoided earlier. "Aunt Theresa, if there's anything else you'd like to know about the stuff Mrs. O'Gara told you yesterday afternoon, I'll be happy to—"

"Yes, well, perhaps after dinner," she interrupted, handing me three plates.

I took them with a questioning look—that she totally ignored. With a sigh, I got out silverware and napkins and carried them with the plates into the dining room. My aunt was just taking a meatloaf out of the oven when I returned to the kitchen.

"Look, Aunt Theresa, I can tell you don't really—"

"Don't forget the water glasses, Marsha. Then you can spoon these mashed potatoes into a serving dish."

Wow, she really, *really* didn't want to talk—or hear—about anything to do with Martians. Like, at all.

During dinner, Uncle Louie brought up the same topic I'd heard people discussing at church this morning. "A lot of folks think that new company, whatever it is, moving its headquarters to Jewel will really turn things around for this town. I sure won't mind if business picks up at the car lot."

Before they'd pissed me off by being rude to Rigel, those three people we'd met in town this afternoon had confirmed what I'd guessed in church about these newcomers. Which made me wonder again how the Council could have failed to tell me about something as big as a whole *Echtran* company coming to Jewel.

True, the Council had been wrapped up with the Grentl thing all last week. And at the two prior meetings, I'd been so obsessed with Rigel getting his memory back it was possible I might have missed a few details. Still, shouldn't I have received a report or something? I *was* the Sovereign, and Jewel *was* my home town.

"I suppose a bit of new blood could be a good thing, as long as these newcomers don't try to change things around here too much." Aunt Theresa shook her head and clucked her tongue. "Melinda, that waitress at the Lighthouse, said they've come from somewhere on the East Coast?"

"It sounded to me like she was just guessing," I said quickly. "I don't think she knew."

Uncle Louie shrugged. "Wherever they're coming from, there must be a lot of them," he said around a mouthful of mashed potato. "Don Billingsley sold three houses just last week. And he said almost every apartment at Diamond View Terrace has been rented. Bet they finally finish that second phase across Ruby Street, the one they started a few years back, now there's so much demand."

My aunt and uncle continued to talk about ways the new company was likely to change things around town. Uncle Louie was mostly optimistic while Aunt Theresa seemed more apprehensive.

I suspected she'd be way more worried if she knew the truth. After dinner I lingered in the kitchen after we finished up the dishes, planning to at least drop a hint, but my aunt kept bustling around, not looking at me.

"Um, Aunt Theresa, I should probably tell you—"

"There, that's the last of the dishes," she interrupted, putting away the glass she'd just dried. I caught a glimpse of her expression—more wary than curious—before she turned away from me to pull a bowl from a lower cabinet.

"I promised Martha Havens three dozen oatmeal walnut cookies for the benefit tomorrow. I'd better start mixing up the batter."

I stood there uncertainly, waiting, but she didn't look at me again. Finally, I shrugged. "Guess I'll go finish my homework."

She nodded, still refusing to meet my eye, so I left the kitchen and went upstairs. That was some serious denial she had going on! But maybe it was just as well I hadn't said anything before finding out more.

As soon as I reached my bedroom I sent a brief message to Kyna on my omni asking about the newcomers. Less than five minutes later she called me.

"I'm glad that you contacted me, Excellency. You are right, of course, that Jewel's newest residents are *Echtran*. I didn't realize so many had already arrived."

"Why wasn't I told about this ahead of time? This whole thing must have been in the works for a while now. Apparently there was even a piece about it in the Indianapolis newspaper!"

"A, ah, majority of the Council felt that there was no need to involve you in the details until they were finalized. A report was to have been sent last week—to all of us—but the Grentl crisis delayed that, among other things."

"Um, this sounds like something I need to know about *now*," I said. "This new company, or whatever it is, is already generating a lot of gossip."

"Agreed." She sounded oddly relieved. "If your schedule

allows, I will request that the Council meet tomorrow evening so that you—and the rest of us—can receive the full report at once."

Since I couldn't think of a higher priority, now that the Grentl were out of the way, I said that would be fine. Then I finally started catching up on all my homework that had accumulated over the past week.

———

The next morning, Aunt Theresa still seemed determined to act like Saturday never happened. She got bowls and cereal out, sliced up a banana for her and Uncle Louie to share, then poured me a glass of orange juice, just like any other weekday morning.

"I have a, ah, thing at the O'Garas' house tonight, but not until after dinner," I said casually as I took the glass from her.

Her brows rose, along with the level of discomfort I felt off her. I was about to reassure her when she turned to Uncle Louie as though I hadn't even spoken.

"This month's water bill was rather high. Do you know if they've raised the rates again?"

He didn't, but she stubbornly stuck to that topic until I had to leave for school. Walking to the bus stop, I almost wondered if *I* was the delusional one, everything at home was so completely unchanged from before.

At school I overheard a few comments about the new "tech company," mainly students repeating their parents' speculations. It was obvious no one knew anything concrete yet, but pretty soon people were bound to start demanding real info. I just hoped whatever cover story the Council had come up with would satisfy them.

I stayed after to watch football practice since I hadn't been able to all last week, what with the Grentl and all. Rigel needed me there occasionally so he could practice compensating for the enhanced strength and speed our bond gave him when I attended his games.

When we parted at the late buses afterward, I promised to let him know whatever I found out tonight as soon as the Council meeting was over.

I'll try to get a recap from my dad, too, once he gets back, he sent as our buses pulled out of the lot. *Then if I ask questions he won't know I got any info from you.*

Good plan.

We'd both agreed to keep our new, hugely increased telepathic range a secret—for a while, anyway.

Aunt Theresa got home not long after I did. "Are you ready?"

I looked up from the kitchen table, where I was finishing the homework I'd started during football practice. "Ready?"

I was pretty sure if she meant ready to finally answer questions about Martian stuff she wouldn't be smiling so broadly.

"To represent Jewel High. I'm sure you want to look your best for those publicity photos."

Oh, right. Those stupid Homecoming Court pictures. "Um, almost. I just need to touch up my lip gloss and brush my hair."

Carrying my books up to my room, I reached out to Rigel again. *Are you doing that promo stuff downtown this afternoon?*

Yeah. Just got out of the shower, so we're heading to town now. You?

Yep. Aunt Theresa just reminded me. Think Trina will be at her dad's store?

Rigel's mental laughter made me smile. *Are you kidding? Not a chance. See you soon, M!*

Though the whole idea of posing for pictures so local store

owners could use us in their advertising seemed lame, at least I'd get to do it with Rigel. Plus I'd be spared seeing a bunch of pics of him in the paper next to Trina, like last year.

Rigel was right—there was no sign of Trina when my aunt and I got to the electronics store twenty minutes later, though both her parents were there. I shared a secret grin with Rigel as I moved to his side where the Court was already lining up for pictures.

Aunt Theresa, meanwhile, was clearly in her element, basking in the reflected glory of my position as Junior Princess.

"I'm sure Marsha was elected because she's such a likable girl," I overheard her confiding to Freshman Princess Andrea Perkins's mom, who sang in the choir with her at church. "Always so helpful around the house."

Like she gave me a choice? To tune her out, I smiled up at Rigel. *I'm already looking forward to the end of football season, when we can spend more time together.*

Me, too. The look he slanted my way made a delicious warmth curl through me. *Everything was so great last fall, before—*

Before all the political stuff got in the way. Now it can finally be like that again.

Even though I'd deliberately avoided Sean's name, both of us involuntarily glanced over to where he and Missie, this year's Homecoming King and Queen, were getting their pictures taken. Aunt Theresa, I noticed, was now exchanging barbed pleasantries with Trina's mom.

"I hope your daughter wasn't too disappointed at not being voted onto the Homecoming Court this year," she was saying, though not loudly enough that anyone without Martian senses was likely to overhear.

Mrs. Squires gave a brittle, tinkling laugh. "While I'm sure you've been gratified to see your niece finally blossom a bit this past year, my Trina has been winning far more important competitions and pageants since she was twelve. Why, the mayor of Jewel himself crowned Trina Cornsilk Queen at this summer's county fair and last year's State fair, as a member of the Miss Soybean court, she shook the Governor's hand."

I saw Aunt Theresa's lips tighten. "Cornsilk Queen? I'll have you know my Marsha was awarded—" She broke off, her cheeks going pinker. From the sudden alarm I detected from her, I could guess what she'd nearly blurted out.

"That is," she continued after a moment. "Marsha has always been far more focused on her academics than on popularity—or boys. It was her friends who worked to have her nominated for Homecoming Court."

"Whatever you say, Theresa. I heard it was a very close contest this year, so unless Marsha and our star quarterback avoid more of their frequent breakups, she's not likely to win a nomination for Homecoming Queen next year. But who knows? She might get lucky again." Mrs. Squires turned away with a smile that reminded me of Trina.

Aunt Theresa glared after her, her earlier alarm at her near-slip now swallowed up by frustration.

Huh. My aunt might not want to talk to *me* about what she'd learned on Saturday, but she was clearly dying to tell other people what a big deal her niece really was. Getting a medal from the President obviously topped being named Cornsilk Queen.

Though I was sure Aunt Theresa was way too sensible to let temptation get the better of her, I really should remind her how important it was to keep everything she'd learned secret. If I could ever get her to listen.

3

Inclusions

"BANNER DAY AT THE LOT," Uncle Louie announced when he got home that night, barely in time for dinner. "It's why I'm so late. At least two dozen customers came in and I personally sold *three* cars—on a Monday!"

He sat down and took a big gulp of iced tea. "A bunch of others promised to come back tomorrow or the next day, said they're planning to buy, too. Didn't I say that company moving its headquarters here was good news? Shoot, if this trend continues, you can quit your extra job at the florist, Theresa."

I glanced at my aunt, who seemed more surprised than happy.

"Wow, that's great, Uncle Louie," I said to make up for her silence. "Three cars!" I was pretty sure his previous record was three in one *week*.

"Did the other salesmen do as well?" Aunt Theresa asked, now looking cautiously pleased.

"Joe sold two and Buddy one—it's just the three of us there on Mondays. But get this—several people asked for me personally! Said I'd been recommended." He beamed at us across the table.

"Recommended?" Aunt Theresa echoed doubtfully. "By whom?"

"Satisfied customers, obviously. Maybe the O'Garas? I heard one guy mention them to his wife. Probably others, too. *Most* people like me, Theresa." He was obviously a little hurt she wasn't more enthusiastic about his triumph.

At mention of the O'Garas, my aunt flicked a glance my way before looking back at Uncle Louie. "Sorry, dear. Of course I'm happy for you—for all of us. I was simply curious. So many people moving to town all at once, well…it's going to take a bit of getting used to. For everyone."

"I'm sure not seeing any downside so far." Uncle Louie scooped up a big forkful of beef stroganoff. "Bring 'em on!"

Most nights Uncle Louie dominated the dinner conversation and tonight was no different, especially since he had so much to talk about. As he went on to describe the cars he'd sold and the people he'd sold them to—including a comment on how good-looking most of the newcomers were—I could sense my aunt's growing uneasiness. She was definitely getting suspicious.

I waited until she and I were putting the dinner dishes in the sink to say, "Aunt Theresa, there's something you should probably know about these new people in town, this company—"

She glanced pointedly at the clock. "Aren't you supposed to be at the O'Garas' by seven-thirty? It's nearly that now. Try not to be any later than you can help, as it's a school night."

With a little sigh of resignation, I nodded. "Right. I'll, um, try to be home as early as I can. G'night Aunt Theresa."

———

When I arrived at the O'Garas,' the entire seven-member *Echtran* Council greeted me by bowing in unison—Kyna, Nara, and Connor holographically, since they didn't live in Jewel. Malcolm and Breann had moved here last spring, and of course Mrs. O'Gara and Mr. Stuart—Rigel's dad and the newest member of the Council—had lived here even longer.

After we all exchanged brief greetings, little Nara as enthusiastically as always, I took the only unoccupied chair.

"Excellency, I suggest we get right to business." Kyna was currently the oldest, most level-headed, and longest-serving member of the Council. She'd taken over as leader after Rigel's grandfather, Shim, left to become my Regent back on Mars. "Connor, you have your report on the status of the new *Echtrans*?"

Nodding, he stood. One of four Royals on the Council, Connor was tall, blond and almost absurdly handsome. Glancing off to one side at something not visible in his holographic image, he began.

"As you know, Excellency, due to your persuasiveness while in Nuath, nearly five thousand of our people emigrated from Mars over the summer—many, many times more than during any previous launch window. With so little time to prepare for such an influx, our first challenge was to arrange lodging for them all in Bailerealta, Dun Cloch and other, smaller, *Echtran* enclaves.

"Our standard orientation training had to be accelerated in order to process them through quickly, thereby making room for newer arrivals. This entailed fabricating an unprecedented number of new identities, records and personal histories before allowing them to leave their *Echtran* compounds to begin their integration into *Duchas* society. Despite those challenges, all has proceeded relatively smoothly thus far, as I stated in my preliminary report last month."

I frowned. "I didn't receive that report."

"No, Excellency." I detected disapproval in the glance Kyna gave Connor and a few of the others. "*Some* here felt that was unnecessary."

Breann, a stunning brunette and, incidentally, another Royal, smiled at me in a way I found slightly condescending. "You already had so many responsibilities to deal with, Excellency. We thought it best not to add to them when this was a matter the Council was well able to handle ourselves, as we have handled all other *Echtran* affairs over the years."

Before they'd discovered I was alive, in other words. I already knew the Royals on the Council weren't nearly as happy as they pretended to be that a sixteen-year-old girl now had authority over them. It wasn't like I'd asked for this job—rather the reverse. But it was mine now, and I was determined to do the best I could.

"While I appreciate your concern," I said, not hiding my sarcasm, "I should have been told right away about something as important as a large number of *Echtrans* suddenly moving to *my* hometown."

"Not so very sudden." Malcolm's smile also seemed irritatingly patronizing. "You may recall, Excellency, that even prior to your trip to Nuath last spring we discussed the establishment of an *Echtran* center of operations here in Jewel, as it is your home. It's why our Council meetings are now held here, and why a small number of *Echtrans* had already relocated to Jewel, to include myself and Breann."

"Of course I remember. But it was presented as something that would happen well in the future—months, even years from now."

"That was the original plan," Breann confirmed. "But we were forced to move more quickly when so many of our new arrivals expressed a desire to live in Jewel."

I blinked. "They did? Why?"

Breann's smile seemed more genuine now. "Because of you, Excellency. You apparently painted such a glowing picture of life in this town that nearly a quarter of those you convinced to relocate requested that Jewel be their new home."

Oops. "I just used it as an example, since it's what I know best. I never meant—" I broke off, frowning. "A quarter? That's over a thousand people! Jewel can't possibly accommodate that many *Echtrans* all at once. There's not room, for one thing."

"Of course not, Excellency," Connor quickly replied. "And not nearly that many are actually moving there. While a large city like New York or Chicago can absorb a few hundred *Echtrans* easily enough, smaller communities—"

"Like Jewel?"

He nodded. "For those, we've had to be more innovative to avoid drawing unwanted attention. Fortunately, some of that groundwork was already laid. Early this year we created a corporation, wholly owned by the *Echtran* community, with the intention of eventually moving its operations and people to Jewel. To that end, some months ago that corporation purchased a defunct factory and a few hundred adjacent acres of unused farmland on the outskirts of town. That property is now being developed well ahead of our original schedule."

"Developed...to do what? I mean, what are we telling people?"

Kyna answered me. "NuAgra's stated purpose is to conduct research into genetically enhancing food crops to increase production and decrease the need for artificial pesticides and fertilizers. Press releases to that effect have already been sent to the local media."

Thus that article in the Indianapolis paper yesterday.

"What will they really be doing? And what if people try to check out that story?" Given the grumblings I'd already heard about "hiring locally," I was sure *someone* would. Maybe a lot of someones. "Won't it look strange that this whole company practically sprang up overnight?"

"Not at all," Breann assured me. "On paper, it appears as

though NuAgra has been in existence for years but has only now chosen to move its headquarters to Jewel in order to expand operations."

"As to your other question," Malcolm said, "*Echtrans* really will be using the facility to develop ways to better provide food for both our own people and the *Duchas*...among other things. The sensitive nature of even their purported research will provide ample justification for secrecy, as well as for bringing in their own, specially trained people as employees."

That so many details had already been worked out was mind-boggling—and irritating. "I absolutely should have been told about all of this *much* sooner."

Connor cleared his throat noisily. "I was in the process of preparing a report that would have been shared with you last week, Excellency, but our priorities rather abruptly, er, changed. At that point the Council felt it would be unwise to distract you with other matters."

I huffed out a breath, only partially mollified by that reasoning. "Okay. So how many people *are* we talking about?"

Again, Connor consulted something I couldn't see. "By the end of the week, one hundred eighty-six new *Echtrans* will have relocated to Jewel."

"One hundred—!" Okay, it wasn't a thousand, but still...

"For now. More will undoubtedly arrive after the next launch window. By then the Jewel *Duchas* should have grown accustomed to the first wave, making integration of subsequent groups even easier."

Jewelites, in my experience, tended to be pretty mistrustful of anything new. The Stuarts and O'Garas had managed to fit in pretty quickly, but Rigel and Sean being star athletes had helped a lot. Which prompted me to ask how many of our new arrivals would be kids.

"Only eleven." Nara spoke for the first time since her initial, effusive greeting. "On my recommendation, families with children younger than twelve years old will remain in purely *Echtran* communities for the present, as youngsters pose a greater security risk."

That made sense. Kids, even teenagers, did tend to blurt things out without thinking. I'd done it plenty of times myself. "So just middle school and high school age?"

"Yes." Nara consulted her tablet. "According to my notes, seven will be attending Jewel High School, ranging in age from fourteen to seventeen. All should be enrolled by the end of this week. If you'd like, I can send you my report on them."

"That would be good, thanks. I take it their parents have already found places to live here in town?"

Malcolm nodded. "Most arranged to buy or rent homes in Jewel as soon as they were approved to come, well before leaving the compounds. NuAgra is also subsidizing the completion, renovation and construction of more housing units to help meet future demand."

Which probably included that Diamond View Terrace addition Uncle Louie had speculated about last night.

I must have still looked concerned, because Connor said, "Not to worry, Excellency. Everyone approved to relocate there underwent rigorous screening before being released from their training compounds. We couldn't risk allowing someone with anti-Royal leanings to move to your community, particularly given that recent, public attack upon you."

Which Rigel had prevented, even though he hadn't yet gotten his memory back at the time.

"Did you ever find out who sent that man after me? Or was he working alone?"

"I'm afraid we weren't able to discover that, Excellency."

Kyna's expression was troubled. "The night before he was to undergo a memory extraction, he was found dead in his cell."

My eyes widened. "Dead? You mean someone killed him before he could talk?"

Kyna grimaced slightly. "Our Healers' preliminary examination indicated he died of natural causes—a heart attack—but the timing…"

"I've been assured there will be a complete investigation and autopsy," Connor said. "If he *was* deliberately silenced, he was likely on an anti-Royal mission, just as he claimed. We know they've resorted to violence before."

I suppressed a shudder. "How did you make sure no anti-Royals are moving here?"

I agreed in principle with what the so-called Populist Movement stood for: equal representation for all Martians. In fact, it was something I hoped to eventually bring about myself. But if they'd actually killed that crazy guy to keep him from talking, they'd lowered themselves to Faxon's level. That dictator—now deposed—had also resorted to violence, intimidation and murder to subdue opposition.

"Nuathan records are quite thorough on some points," Breann assured me. "Thanks, ironically, to Faxon. He kept careful track of anyone outspoken about their Royalist sympathies. The very people he most sought to oppress are the safest ones to have living here."

Traditionalists, then—which I also had mixed feelings about. Back on Nuath they'd been my first supporters, but also the first to turn against me when the news about Rigel broke.

"That probably explains the attitudes of the three I met downtown yesterday," I muttered.

"I hope they did nothing inappropriate." Kyna raised an eyebrow. "We required those relocating to Jewel to undergo additional training to minimize the chances of that, should they first encounter you in a public setting. One reason they were among the last to be released from the compounds."

"Well, they didn't bow or squeal or anything," I told her, "but they were downright rude to Rigel—which seemed pretty inappropriate to me, considering he helped save the freaking *world* Friday night! Is it possible not everyone has read your statement yet?"

Malcolm shifted in his chair, averting his eyes from mine. At the same time, I felt discomfort emanating from Breann and Mrs. O. Immediately, I was suspicious.

"You *did* send out that bulletin Saturday explaining how we stopped the Grentl, right?"

"A report was sent, Excellency." Kyna's expression was distinctly disapproving as it swept over the four Royals. "However the Council voted, four to three, to edit out several, ah, details first."

"What details? You told me the whole story about what Rigel and I did—*together*—would go out over MARSTAR and the Nuathan networks."

Malcolm cleared his throat. "We were all rather caught up in the moment Saturday afternoon, when we first learned the Grentl were leaving. It's possible we, er, implied we would release more information than was wise. Something we realized after a more sober evaluation."

"If you don't mind, I'd like to see *exactly* what was sent out." After everything they'd done to Rigel and me, I should have *known* better than to trust the Council Royals.

"Oh. Um, of course." Breann punched the text up on her tablet, then handed it to me.

With growing indignation, I read:

"Nuathans and *Echtrans* will be happy to learn that the threat so recently posed by those aliens known as the Grentl has been averted. Unprecedented collaboration between Martian Scientists in Nuath and on Earth allowed us to counter the Grentl electromagnetic pulse with a precisely-timed positron beam, resulting in the colorful display Earthbound *Echtrans* undoubtedly noticed. The *Duchas* have been told the fictitious sunspots previously reported to their media created an unusually intense display of "Northern Lights." Our Scientists were assisted in their efforts by our new Sovereign, who learned important details about the Grentl plan via her communications with them. Her diplomacy also resulted in the Grentl withdrawal from solar space. The *Echtran* Council extends its gratitude to Sovereign Emileia for her help in preventing what could have been a terrible catastrophe by exhibiting yet again that she has the qualities necessary to lead our people into a brighter future."

Practically flinging the tablet back at Breann, I glared around the room. "Rigel's name wasn't even *mentioned!* He risked his life every bit as much as I did!"

"We, ah, were concerned that our people might be unnecessarily upset by hearing how close they came to losing another Sovereign." Breann's tone was placating, but I wasn't placated in the least.

"So you decided to play down my role and not mention Rigel's at *all*? The President of the United States—a *Duchas*—knows more about what really happened than our own people do!"

Malcolm frowned. "Kyna assured us that the President has sworn absolute secrecy as to the precise—"

"That's not the point and you know it!"

Mrs. O, who'd been quiet all evening, leaned forward. "Excellency—M—try to calm down, do. Most of us felt certain our people would be more reassured by a Scientific explanation than with some fantastical-seeming story about *graell* bonds."

Though she spoke soothingly, I sensed both irritation and resentment—probably because she still hadn't forgiven me for getting back together with Rigel. In her view I'd jilted her son, my "destined Consort," to be with my non-Royal boyfriend—and had hurt Sean in the process. Even if Sean now understood how important it was that Rigel and I be together, I didn't think Sean's mother ever would, not really.

"You know—all of you know—I could *never* have stopped the Grentl without Rigel. Without our bond." I was still furious. "Why do you keep trying to pretend it doesn't exist?"

"Of course we're grateful to young Stuart for the role he played," Connor allowed. "We've already sent an official letter of thanks to him, on behalf of the Council."

"Grateful!" I snorted. "Yet you're willing to let people believe that nasty *Echtran Enquirer* article full of lies about him?"

I turned to Mr. Stuart. "You said a few days ago you'd received some nasty emails threatening Rigel. Have there been any more?"

He grimaced slightly. "More insults than threats. I, ah, haven't told Ariel or Rigel about them. They'd had enough stress already."

"See?" I demanded, turning back to the Council. "Rigel risked his life for you but you're willing to let him be a target for any crazy traditionalists moving here who consider him a threat to our future. What kind of gratitude is that?"

This time it was Breann who tried to calm me down. "You must understand, Excellency, that this is still a difficult time of transition for our people. While they are relieved to have Faxon gone and the monarchy restored, the recently discovered power depletion in Nuath has shaken them badly, not to mention learning about the Grentl. It is more important than ever that they retain confidence in the Royal line—and their born Sovereign."

"Not at the expense of Rigel's safety," I insisted.

"Perhaps a security detail—?" Malcolm suggested.

"That won't change what people think about him." I imagined the new students at school making snide comments to his face, having no idea how much they owed him. "Send another message, this time with the full story of what Rigel did to protect them. It's the only fair thing to do and you know it."

Nara nodded, then Kyna, but the Royals still looked stubborn.

"If we do that, we'll have to reveal *how* you and Stuart stopped the EMP," Malcolm pointed out. "That would include details about the potentially lethal electrical bolts you and he are able to produce. Surely you don't want your subjects to grow afraid of you?"

Breann and Connor and Mrs. O all murmured their agreement with that argument but I refused to back down.

"Figure out a way to word it so you don't scare people, then. Because if you don't issue a statement in the next day or two, I will. I imagine Mr. Stuart and Shim will both be willing to make sure it reaches everyone."

"Hm. Yes, Excellency, now that you mention it, perhaps that would be best." Malcolm glanced at Mrs. O.

"I agree." She also seemed oddly pleased with the idea. "If you write the statement yourself, Excellency, there can be no question of the Council inadvertently upsetting you again by our phrasing. A very good suggestion, Malcolm."

"Fine," I snapped.

Giving Rigel full credit was the surest way to keep him safe *and* finally get all Martians to accept us as a couple. With all these new *Echtrans* coming to Jewel, including students at school who'd encounter Rigel and me on a regular basis, that was more important than ever.

I was determined to have that statement written before I went to bed tonight.

When I got home, just a couple minutes past nine o'clock, Uncle Louie was dozing in front of the TV and Aunt Theresa was doing a crossword puzzle. She looked up quickly when I poked my head into the living room, her expression—and emotions—betraying her curiosity.

I thought sure she'd ask about the meeting, but after staring at me for a second, she just said, "I'm glad they didn't keep you too late. Is all of your homework done?"

"Oh. Um, almost. I'll...get right on that."

I lingered for another moment in case she really did want to ask me anything, but she turned back to her crossword. With a little shrug, I headed upstairs.

Though I wanted to get started on that statement right away, I first reached out for Rigel with my mind. *Hey, are you there? Can you talk?*

Sure. Just a sec, he sent back a few heartbeats later.

Since his parents didn't know we could communicate from this far away, he probably needed to get someplace away from his mom so she wouldn't guess what was going on.

While I waited, I pulled some books out of my backpack and spread them on my desk so it would look like I really was doing homework if Aunt Theresa happened to check on me. Not that I expected her to, the way she'd been acting lately. I'd written and scratched out three different opening sentences to my statement when Rigel's voice sounded in my mind.

Okay, I'm in my room now. What's the deal? Oops, sounds like Dad just got home. Back in a few, okay?

Though frustrated at the delay, I didn't argue. I had time to write and scratch out two whole paragraphs before Rigel finally came back.

Sorry, Dad wanted to tell Mom and me all about the meeting. Wow, nearly two hundred new Echtrans *coming to town? He sure didn't hint there'd be that many this morning!* I could sense Rigel was as taken aback by the number as I'd been.

It sounded like some of the Council only got the details tonight.

But this had to be in the works for a while, right? he asked, just like I had.

Some of it was, but they claimed they didn't know for sure how many were coming until a week or so ago. And that was right when—

All hell broke loose, he finished for me.

Yeah. So they decided not to say anything about the newcomers last week because they didn't want to distract me.

Maybe a good call, considering?

I wasn't nearly as ready to absolve the Council. *Maybe. I still think they should have told me. And there's more.*

Uh-oh, Mom's calling me. We can talk more tomorrow at school if we don't get another chance tonight, okay?

Okay, I sent back reluctantly. *Love you!*

Love you, too, M!

His presence in my mind disappeared and I let out a frustrated sigh, feeling slightly drained. Long-distance telepathy took a lot more effort than when we were closer, so maybe waiting till we were face to face to tell him the rest would be better.

Rigel was bound to be even more upset than I was that the Council hadn't mentioned him in their statement. If I could show him at least a draft of my follow-up, he'd know the omission was temporary, which might help. I got back to work.

But no matter how I worded my description of what really happened Friday night, it sounded like I was either tooting my own horn or giving Rigel top billing—which I *knew* he wouldn't allow. I was mostly okay with the Council singing our praises but it felt super weird and awkward for me to do it myself.

I suddenly realized that Malcolm and Mrs. O must have foreseen this exact problem—which would explain why they were so eager to have *me* write the follow-up statement I'd demanded.

Finally, rubbing my tired eyes, I gave it up for the evening. Tomorrow I'd talk it over with Rigel. Together, I was sure we could come up with something both accurate and (relatively) humble. We had to.

4

Cleavage

THE NEXT MORNING I came down to breakfast a little early in case my aunt was finally ready to listen only to discover she'd already left for the elementary school where she taught—a full half hour earlier than usual.

"She said she had papers to grade or something like that," Uncle Louie told me when I asked. "Oh, hey, if you're making toast, make me a piece, too."

I was sure Aunt Theresa had really left early to avoid talking to me, but there was nothing I could do about it now. I got out another piece of bread and put it into the toaster.

"Mum told us this morning how many new *Echtrans* are coming to Jewel," Molly whispered excitedly when she and Sean joined me at the bus stop a little later. "Sean and I already knew about NuAgra, of course, but didn't realize it would be that big."

"Yeah, definitely more people than I expected." I tried not to show how irked I was that they'd been told more ahead of time than I had. I mean, I *was* the Sovereign.

"Hope these people have been a lot better briefed on how to act than some of the, uh, tourists we've had," Sean said.

"Kyna said the ones coming here got extra briefings." I didn't mention the three I'd met on Sunday.

Sean dropped his voice lower, since the two sophomores from our stop were headed our way. "That's good. But if any seem at all out of line, you can count on me—and Molly, of course—to run interference. Keep them from getting too close or…whatever."

I smiled up at him. "Thanks, Sean. Hope that won't be necessary, but it's good to know you guys have my back." I infused all the gratitude I could into my voice, hoping to ease some of the lingering hurt I still sensed from him. It seemed to help a tiny bit.

When our bus left the outskirts of town to trundle through the cornfields I reached out for Rigel, since we hadn't "said" much more than goodnight to each other before I fell asleep last night. *Are you at school yet?*

Just got here. What's up?

Hoping we can talk before class, that's all. Meet you out front in a couple minutes, okay?

He was waiting near the curb when our bus pulled up and greeted me with a quick kiss as soon as Sean's back was turned. It bothered him, too, that Sean was having trouble adjusting to us being a couple again.

"So?" he said, linking hands as we turned toward the school. "What did you want to talk about? More stuff about these newcomers?"

"Not exactly." Keeping my voice to the sub-whisper only he could hear, I quickly told him about the "edited" report the Council sent out Saturday. I got pissed all over again as I spoke but Rigel took the news surprisingly calmly.

"It's not that big a deal, M. Seriously." Just like on Sunday, he wasn't nearly as upset as I was.

"It doesn't bother you? Really?"

"Not much. It's enough—more than enough—that I helped keep you alive and safe. Along with, y'know, the rest of the world." He grinned. "It's awkward enough at school and around town when people treat me like some kind of hero just because of football. This would make me feel even weirder."

Together, we entered the school. "I get that. I do. I feel awkward when people treat me so differently because of the whole Sovereign thing, too. Still, it's not fair they didn't give you credit when you were a *real* hero."

"Sounds like you didn't get as much credit as you should have, either. But hey, if the Scientists want to be the heroes, I say we let them. If keeping a low profile means we can be together without an audience more often, I'll take that trade in a heartbeat."

He leaned in for another kiss as we reached my locker, which distracted me for a few seconds. But only a few.

"I don't know, Rigel. You saw what happened downtown Sunday. I was really counting on that statement to change people's minds, prove to them we *have* to be together. I'm worried if we don't do something to counteract all the lies that have been spread, what happened back in Nuath could start happening here. Especially with all these new *Echtrans* coming to Jewel—"

"It'll be fine, M. You'll see. We'll just have to prove it to them a little more slowly, that's all."

"No, that's part of what I wanted to tell you." The warning bell rang, so I spoke more quickly. "Last night I insisted the Council send out another statement, telling what *really* happened, and they said I could write it myself. I've already started a rough draft." Several, in fact, but I didn't say that. "I was thinking you could help me make it better, less awkward. Then—"

His frown stopped me. "I don't know, M. Let's talk this through before you do anything we can't take back, okay?"

"Um, okay." I was confused and a little disappointed by his reluctance. "Lunch in the courtyard? We can talk more then."

As the morning went on, I tried to discreetly tap into Rigel's thoughts to figure out why he was so resistant to setting people straight. But all I picked up were a few memories from last week and a growing sense of determination. Surely over lunch, when we could again talk face to face, he'd tell me what was really going on.

"So," I said as soon as we were seated on the stone bench with our sandwiches. "Have you thought more about what my statement should say?" Thankfully, the courtyard was deserted, even though it was sunny and not too hot after Sunday's rain.

The look he gave me was wary—and worried. "Yeah, M, I have. And…I don't think you should send one at all."

"What? Of course I should! Why would you say that? Do you *want* those crazy ultra-traditionalists bad-mouthing you—or worse? Remember what they did to you in Nuath? And that threatening note your mom got—?"

"I remember." He put his hand over mine, trying to calm me. "But that threat was about me getting my memory back, which is a done deal now. Everybody already knows about it. Anyway, I'd much rather deal with a few insults from people who don't know any better than risk them trying to separate us again."

I stared at him. "But don't you see? That's exactly why—"

"No. Think. Remember how the Council and even some of the Scientists reacted when we generated those electrical bolts for their tests? They were scared. Shoot, *we* were scared! Some Council members even argued we should be kept apart so we couldn't accidentally hurt anyone. Do you really want *everyone* to know what we can do? How do you think the *Echtran Enquirer* will spin *that?*"

The Council Royals had said something similar last night, I recalled.

"Didn't Shim already publicize what those Scientists found out about our *graell* bond, at least in Nuath? We haven't gotten flack over that. Why should this be any worse?"

"He didn't share that part. Dad told me. Just the genetic affinity stuff and a hint about our mental link. Besides, according to my folks people were so busy freaking out about the Grentl, nobody paid much attention anyway."

I let out a little huff of frustration. "Yeah, but now that the Grentl are gone people will be looking for new gossip, you know they will. We don't have to say we were heroes. That'll sound weird coming from us, anyway. But can't we at least tell everyone it was our bond that kept the Grentl from carrying out their plan?"

"How, without mentioning the electrical thing? Really, M, I think we should just let it go, at least for now. See if any of the stuff you're worried about actually materializes. Anyway, we should eat. Lunch is almost over." He unwrapped my tuna sandwich and handed it to me.

I kept arguing with Rigel—silently—for the rest of the day but he refused to budge. He was convinced the risks outweighed the possible problems. I knew he'd feel differently if he thought another statement would make *me* safer, but the one most likely to suffer from us *not* saying anything was him—which didn't give me much leverage.

I could tell he was starting to get irritated when he made me promise not to distract him during football practice. I decided to just go home so I'd be less tempted to break that promise—and because I was getting irritated, too, and hated being on the outs with Rigel about anything.

My frustration over Rigel's stubbornness made me even more determined to make Aunt Theresa talk about the whole Martian thing. I even rehearsed an opening for when she got home, but she didn't give me a chance to use it.

"If you've finished your homework, Marsha, you need to run over to the antique store to have your photo taken," my aunt said as she walked in, without so much as a hello.

I frowned. "Just me?"

"Yes, they're doing individual pictures rather than the Court as a group. Scheduling issues, they said."

Maybe if I got it over with quickly, there'd still be time to make Aunt Theresa listen. Taking my bike since that was faster than walking, I headed over to Duncan's Antiques on Topaz Street. I touched base with Rigel on the way, hoping he could meet me there, but he'd already made plans to go later. So I couldn't keep pestering him?

It turned out Mr. Duncan only wanted to snap a picture and ask me a few questions, so I was back home less than twenty minutes after I left. Plenty of time to help Aunt Theresa snap the peas for dinner...and get her talking. This time I planned to try an indirect approach.

"I was thinking maybe we should tell Uncle Louie about, y'know, everything this evening," I suggested, sitting down at the kitchen table with my bowl of rinsed peas. "I know on Saturday I said we shouldn't, but now, with all these new people coming to Jewel—"

My aunt turned from the stove looking startled. "Tell—? I'm sure I can't imagine anything we'd say to him about...anything. Especially considering that your uncle has never been known for his discretion. Why, even back in high school—" She broke off, shaking her head.

"I really think he should know."

After his record-breaking sales day yesterday, it occurred to me that some of the newcomers might try to use my aunt and uncle—and friends—to curry influence. I'd seen enough of that sort of thing back in Nuath to know *Echtrans* weren't above such tactics.

"You don't know him as well as I do, Marsha." Aunt Theresa turned away from me. Again. "If a situation arises where it becomes important, we can tell him then. For now, I would prefer not to."

I huffed out a frustrated breath. "Obviously, since you won't even talk about it yourself. How can you—?"

"That's enough, Marsha. Are those peas ready yet?"

"Almost," I grumped, even though I'd barely started them. Much as I wanted to make her talk to me, years of habit kept me from pushing when she used that tone. I let it drop. Again.

When Uncle Louie got home he was nearly as upbeat as the night before, crowing that he'd sold two more cars that day. I was half-tempted to defy my aunt and just blurt out the truth to him, but I didn't. Even though I now doubted it would be possible—or safe—to keep him in the dark indefinitely.

***

Aunt Theresa was in the kitchen like usual when I came downstairs the next morning, but she seemed as determined as ever to act like everything was perfectly normal. At first, anyway.

"About time," Uncle Louie exclaimed as I poured my orange juice. "They've finally printed something in the local paper about that new company. Sounds like the mayor's taking all the credit for getting them here," he added with a chuckle. "No big surprise, since he's up for reelection this fall."

He went on to read part of the article aloud. The description of the research NuAgra would be doing to increase crop production and decrease reliance on pesticides and fertilizers was almost verbatim what I'd been told by the Council Monday night. Taken straight from their press release, I assumed.

When Aunt Theresa glanced my way as he read, I raised my eyebrows and nodded significantly. The alarm I'd already sensed from her increased, but then she turned away to begin slicing a banana with mathematical precision.

I sighed.

"Did you see the article about NuAgra in this morning's paper?" I asked Molly at the bus stop a little while later. Sean was apparently getting a ride to school with a buddy, as he did more often than not these days.

She shook her head. "We don't get the local one. What did it say?"

"The exact same story the Council told me they were putting out for public consumption. Uncle Louie thinks it's great but I doubt everyone in Jewel will feel the same. Especially since they're not hiring."

"Mum and dad were talking about that last night. Hope it won't—" She broke off as the bus rounded the corner and the other two kids from our stop came jogging up.

We clearly weren't the only ones excited—and a little apprehensive—about so many new people moving to Jewel. It was already the main topic of conversation when we boarded the bus and when my friends Bri and Deb got on a few stops later, they immediately joined the discussion.

"My dad says we're getting *eight* new students at school tomorrow," Bri announced as they slid into the seat across the aisle from Molly and me. "They're supposed to be registering today."

"Eight? Really?" Nara's report had only named seven.

Bri misunderstood my surprise. "I know! Wacky, right? It was a huge deal to get three last year."

All of whom were also *Echtrans*, though of course Bri didn't know that.

"He says the middle school is getting two or three new kids, too," she said. "How awesome would it be if we got another sports phenom like Rigel or Sean?"

She was obviously joking but that actually wasn't unlikely at all, since *Echtrans* tended to be stronger, faster and smarter than the average Earth human.

"Yeah, that *would* be awesome," Molly agreed with a grin when I hesitated. "Then it wouldn't all be on Rigel and Sean to prop up their teams."

"Not that I'm holding my breath," Bri said. "I mean, how many more can there be out there like Sean and Rigel?"

Not only had Rigel completely revitalized our football program last fall, Sean had taken our formerly-lame basketball team to State last spring. They were both dramatically better than any other athletes at our little rural school, but were they above average for Martians? I suddenly realized I had no idea.

Rigel met me at my locker. "People were going nuts on my bus about the NuAgra thing this morning," he murmured as we walked to Pre-Cal.

"Mine, too. It *is* pretty big news for a town and school this small. That'd be true even if they weren't, y'know—" *Aliens,* I finished silently.

He slanted an amused glance down at me. "Tell me you don't still think of us that way?"

"Duh. Of course *I* don't. But if other people knew, what would *they* think?" Aunt Theresa, for example.

"Good point. We all just need to make sure that doesn't happen."

"*All* is right. I hope these new kids paid attention during that extra training the Council—"

I broke off as Matt Mullins, one of Rigel's teammates, caught up with us.

"So, didja hear? All those new students are supposed to be starting classes tomorrow."

We both nodded. "Do you know anything about them?" I was curious how different sections of the gossip mill were spinning things.

"Not really," Matt said, "but I think I saw one of them in the office when I went past it just now. At least I hope so, because wowza! She was gorgeous. Her mom was pretty easy on the eyes, too." He waggled his eyebrows.

It was announced during first period that the new students would all be registering today, so between classes that was almost the only thing people talked about. Even the teachers seemed excited when they told us, in both Chemistry and Lit, to expect new classmates the next day.

As the day went on, everyone who managed to catch a glimpse of one of the newcomers registering made a point of reporting back to their friends.

"O. M. G," I overheard Amber saying to the other cheerleaders at lunch. "I am *so* glad it was my day to help in the office second period. Four of the new students are guys and *every one* of them is to die for! I don't know if I'm going to be able to handle so much gorgeousness in school every day." She fanned herself vigorously.

The others immediately started peppering her with questions, but I stopped listening when Bri, Deb and Molly joined Rigel and me at our table. All three were speculating excitedly about the newcomers, though I assumed Molly's curiosity was for a different reason than Bri's and Deb's.

Or maybe not. "No kidding, Bri," she said as they set down

their trays. "I saw two of the new guys earlier—I think they might be twins?—and wow. Wish I knew what year they are and what classes they'll have."

It occurred to me that Molly hadn't really been around any *Echtran* boys except Sean and Rigel since leaving Bailerealta a year ago. No wonder she was looking forward to meeting a few more.

Maybe Sean will connect with one of the new girls, too, Rigel sent, picking up on my thought.

I glanced over to where Sean was sitting with some of his basketball teammates from last year. *Yeah, that would be really nice.*

If nothing else, it would help me feel a little less guilty over what I'd inadvertently put him through over the past year.

5

Clarity

AFTER LUNCH, our Government teacher said we'd also be getting two new students in there. "So take this time to work with your partners to put the finishing touches on your projects, as they're due Friday and I'd rather not leave our new arrivals with nothing to do tomorrow."

As soon as we paired off, I apologized again to Molly for leaving her in the lurch on our project all of last week.

"Seriously, M, it's fine," she assured me. "What you were doing was like a million times more important than some report about the Constitution. Speaking of which, how is your aunt handling everything, now it's been a few days?"

"I'm not sure," I admitted. "It's like she's pretending that conversation with Kyna and your mom never happened—I mean, she won't refer to it at *all*. I don't get it. If it were me, I'd want to know *everything*."

"Your Aunt Theresa is *so* not you, M," Molly pointed out. "Maybe she just can't wrap her mind around it yet."

"Yeah. Dr. Stuart said she might need time to get used to the idea, but still…" I shook my head, tired of puzzling over it. "So, are you sure there's not *something* I can still do on this project?"

There really wasn't—she'd double-checked the footnotes and everything—so we mostly spent our time speculating about the new students. By now, I was as curious about them as everyone else in school.

In Econ, Trina and Amber seemed to be hatching a whispered plot with a couple of other cheerleaders to set themselves up as some kind of official welcoming committee. I had to laugh, remembering how she'd acted toward Rigel, and then Sean, when they'd arrived at Jewel High last year.

"What's so funny, Marsha?" Trina sniped in response to my chuckle. "You think just because you convinced Rigel and the O'Garas you're something special these new students will, too? News flash. Anyone coming from the East Coast is going to have *way* higher standards."

A year ago that would have embarrassed me into silence. Not now. "Uh-huh. I'm sure if they'd been here last week, it would have made all the difference in the Homecoming Court vote." I knew it still rankled badly that I'd beaten her out for Junior Princess.

She glared at me. "Just wait, Marsha. We're going to be so charming, these new guys won't even *look* at you."

It would actually be great if she was right—but I was pretty sure she wasn't.

"Okay, folks, we've got one heck of a story to cover," Angela, our editor-in-chief, announced in Publications last period, practically rubbing her hands together with glee.

"This corporation moving its headquarters to Jewel is the biggest news this town has seen in years—maybe decades. We may just be an online school newspaper, but we can still do a better job reporting on it than the local rag. The office already gave me the names and class years of all the new students."

She brandished a sheet of paper, then read from it. "Two seniors, Kira Morain and Alan Dempsey. Two juniors, Lucas and Liam Walsh, brothers. Two sophomores, Grady Quinlan and Erin Campbell, and two freshmen, Adina Morain and Jana Blair. Since there are eight of us and eight of them, we'll interview one apiece."

Becky waved a hand in the air. "Ooh, can I have one of the guys?" She and the three other girls on the staff giggled.

Angela frowned them down. "I'll take Alan Dempsey, since we're both seniors. Becky, you can have Kira Morain."

Ignoring Becky's pout, Angela continued, "Rigel, you and M take the Walsh brothers. Jeremy, Grady Quinlan is yours. And you three can decide between you who gets Erin, Jana and Adina."

According to Nara's report on the new students, their being so evenly balanced by both class year and gender was no coincidence, but part of the selection process—though Adina had been listed as an eighth grader instead of ninth. Probably a last-minute change.

"I'll want a full profile on each one, including as much on their parents as you can get. Oh, and if anyone can score an interview with the CEO of NuAgra, you'll be my hero. I've called half a dozen times today but can't get through their voicemail system. Maybe it's not working yet."

Rigel glanced at me. *One of us should probably do that, don't you think? Then we can spin things however seems safest.*

Good plan, I agreed. *I'll give the Council a heads-up.*

Angela went on to suggest we all wrap up any stories already in progress so we could devote next week to the new students— who also needed to be warned before they started giving interviews.

I added that to my lengthening list of mental notes.

If I'd expected a break from Jewel's big news in taekwondo class that afternoon, I was wrong.

"I'm expecting two or three new students on Saturday, maybe more," Master Parker announced with a big smile as soon as we bowed in. "I personally talked with several of the new families, pointing out what a great way this would be to get plugged to their new community. It'll also benefit you people to have new sparring partners. There are flyers on the front desk for you to take on your way out. Feel free to give them to your new classmates at school."

During class I tried hard to focus, to put other concerns out of my mind, like Master Parker always told us to do. But I couldn't help thinking one reason he'd had such an easy time persuading parents to sign their kids up was because they'd heard *I* studied taekwondo.

Which would be awkward even if these kids had already learned to compensate for being stronger and faster than the *Duchas* they were supposed to mimic. I was extra glad now that no children younger than twelve had been permitted to come to Jewel.

When I walked past Burrell's Feed & Seed on my way home, I discovered one more reason to worry. Two employees were taking a smoke break outside the entrance—and talking about NuAgra.

"—put us out of business," I heard one say.

The other man nodded. "Yeah, I saw. Gonna make half the stuff we sell here obsolete, sounds like. Bad enough they're only taking on their own people. Now this."

Wondering how pervasive attitudes like that were already becoming, I walked faster. I needed to message Kyna and request a meeting with *all* the newcomers as soon as possible. Maybe together we could deal with issues like these before they developed into real problems.

When I got home a few minutes later, I was surprised to find Aunt Theresa already in the kitchen—and radiating tension.

"You're home early," I said cautiously as I went to the fridge to pour myself a glass of milk. "Is, um, something wrong?"

Standing up from the stack of papers she'd been grading on the kitchen table, she regarded me with an apprehensive frown. "Not…wrong, precisely, but I'd, ah, like to ask you something. If you don't mind."

Finally! Even though it would delay my message to Kyna, I smiled encouragingly. "Of course I don't mind. I'll tell you whatever you want to know."

She sat back down at the table, so I put the milk away and sat across from her, taking a sip from my glass. And waiting.

For a long moment she fidgeted, shuffling her papers while conflicting emotions played across her face, before blurting out, "This new company, these new people. They're not…they can't really all be—?"

"Yes. That's what I've been trying to tell you. They're people like me. And the O'Garas."

Her eyes widened slightly, then she nodded. "I was afraid that was the case after reading the article in today's paper. I'd hoped— But I suppose it was foolish of me to think that if I ignored the, er, situation it would somehow go away, or at least not matter."

"I'm, sorry, Aunt Theresa. I know it's been a lot for you to take in. Dr. Stuart said I should give you time, wait till you were ready to talk about it."

She huffed out a breath. "Yes. Well. Whether I'm ready or not, I'd best know exactly what Jewel is up against."

Now I frowned. "Up against? What do you mean? It's not an invasion."

One gray eyebrow went up. "Isn't it?"

"Of course not! They're just coming here to…to live their lives, like everyone else."

"But why Jewel?"

I bit my lip. "Um, because of me, mostly. There wasn't time on Saturday for Kyna and Mrs. O'Gara to give you more than the absolute basics, but you remember them telling you I'm their Sovereign, right?"

"Yes, but I'm still not sure I understand what that means. They said your grandfather was killed on…on Mars…by some dictator who also killed your parents here on Earth? But you escaped?"

I nodded. "I'm not sure exactly how, since I was only two, but Shim—that's Rigel's grandfather, my Regent back on Mars—he thinks my parents knew Faxon's people were after them. Apparently they hid me, then made it look like I was with them when they were killed in an arranged accident."

"And they—these, ah, people of yours—only recently discovered you survived?"

"Shim suspected it sooner but it wasn't until the Stuarts moved here that anyone knew for sure *I* was the missing Princess. Believe me, Aunt Theresa, I was just as shocked as you when they told me! It took me a while to believe it, too."

She stared at me for several seconds, like she was trying to see anything remotely "royal" about me—and mostly failing. "I almost wish I still didn't know. I'm not at all comfortable lying to people. Especially in church."

"I'm sorry, Aunt Theresa. But you get why, right? There's no way most Earth people—especially in a little town like Jewel—are ready to know about all this. They might want to…to round us all up and put us in a concentration camp or something."

"I suppose. But what will that new company really be doing? Anything dangerous?"

"No, not at all," I quickly assured her. "NuAgra really will be doing agricultural research, just like the paper said—though their research will probably be a little more, um, high tech than they let on."

My aunt looked slightly relieved—but only slightly. "How many…Martians *are* there on Earth? Total?"

Bracing myself for her reaction, I answered, "About fifteen thousand now, counting the ones that just came here over the summer. It was only about ten thousand before that."

"Only—" she repeated faintly, her earlier tension spiking into alarm. "How big *is* that colony on Mars?"

"There are still almost a quarter of a million people in Nuath. They're starting to run out of power, though, so we're trying to convince as many as possible to move to Earth over the next few decades. Not to take over or anything. They're nothing to be scared of, I promise. They're just…people. You've known Mrs. O'Gara for nearly a year now and you like her, right?"

Grudgingly, she nodded. "Yes. I never would have guessed Lili could be—" She broke off, shaking her head. "And the Stuarts? How many others have been living in Jewel with no one suspecting?"

"Until now, only a few. I don't think you've met any others—except maybe Mr. Cormac."

She blinked. "Jewel High's new vice principal?"

"Yeah. He's also my, er, Bodyguard. It's why he's renting that room over Mrs. Crabtree's garage, across the street."

"Bodyguard? Does that mean you're still in danger? Is that dictator still trying to have you…killed?" Her earlier tension surged back.

"No, no! It's just protocol for the Sovereign to have a Body-guard, like the President has the Secret Service. Faxon was completely overthrown last December and has been in a super secure prison—on Mars—ever since."

She was still frowning. "But before that? What did he do when he found out you were alive?"

I hesitated. I didn't want to scare her, but I also didn't want to lie to her any more.

"Uh, do you remember how we almost got in an accident on the way home from last year's Homecoming game? One of Faxon's people rigged Uncle Louie's car so it wouldn't stop."

"They tampered with our *car*?" she gasped.

"Yes, but they caught him that same night! Okay, a few more bad guys did come after me the next day, but Rigel's family and some others fought them and we, um…won. Nobody's trying to hurt me now." As far as I knew, anyway.

"But…the, er, President said something about you risking your life Friday night?"

"Well, yeah, but that had nothing to do with Faxon."

"No, that woman who came here with the President said something about…another kind of alien? Different from you, I mean."

"I'm *not* an alien, Aunt Theresa. Kyna and Mrs. O'Gara both explained to you how we're all human, descended from a colony those other, different aliens planted on Mars centuries ago. We—"

"Yes, yes, I remember." Now she sounded a bit testy, more like herself, which oddly made me feel a little better. "So what, exactly, *did* you do to deserve that medal?"

"It's…kind of complicated. Those other aliens came here plan-ning to wipe out all technology on Earth with a massive electro-magnetic pulse. We told the media it was sunspots so people wouldn't freak out about an alien attack. Because it *would* have been like a huge solar storm, only way worse. At the last minute,

Rigel and I managed to create a, uh, power surge that sort of turned their EMP back on itself so it never reached Earth."

"But it sounded as though you could have been killed?"

I shrugged, trying to play it down. "That's what the Scientists said. We did get knocked out for a few seconds—the feedback blew up a piece of Martian equipment right near us—but we're both fine now. And those aliens left our solar system the very next day. Really, Aunt Theresa, there's *nothing* to be afraid of now."

For a long moment she just sat there, trying to make sense of it all. "I don't suppose…was that the explosion everyone was talking about on Sunday?"

"Um…yeah. The cornfield by the school seemed like a safe place to set up the equipment, since it needed to be secret and we didn't want to risk anyone else getting hurt."

Though she slowly shook her head, her eyes never leaving my face, I was glad to sense her fear finally receding as curiosity crept back in.

"Lili said you traveled to Mars last spring instead of to Ireland, difficult as that is to believe. Is that where you were involved in the auto accident I was told about?"

"I actually did go to Ireland first, then left for Mars from there. But once I got there some people, ah, didn't want me to leave again. They started a rumor back here that I'd died in a car wreck so you wouldn't ask too many questions. I wasn't *really* in an accident. And I finally managed to convince them I could do my job from here."

I was leaving out a whole lot but she didn't need to hear any more scary details—especially involving people she'd trusted.

"But you're only sixteen. Surely you're not really expected to…to *lead* all of those people?"

"Well, I do have a Regent back on Mars, Rigel's grandfather. He's taking care of all the government stuff there. And the

Echtran Council was already handling that sort of thing on Earth, before they found out I was alive."

That they obviously wanted to *keep* doing so was an issue I still needed to tackle.

"And how does school fit into all of this? What does your being a…a Sovereign entail, exactly?"

"It *has* sometimes been tricky juggling school and all my other commitments without making you suspicious," I admitted. "It'll be easier now I don't have to pretend I'm building Homecoming floats when I'm really dealing with *Echtran* Scientists or have sleepovers at Molly's every time it looks like a Council meeting will go late."

My aunt abruptly pushed away from the table and stood. "I believe that will do for now. Thank you, Marsha. Or…may I still call you Marsha?"

"Sure. It's what everyone still calls me at school—that and M. I'm still the same person I've always been, Aunt Theresa. Nothing needs to change here at home. Not much, anyway." I did hope she might cut me a break on my chores, a little.

"Hmph. Well. In that case, you should probably go upstairs and do your homework. Your, ah, people mustn't have a poorly educated Sovereign."

"Right. Good point."

Heading up to my room, I grinned to myself, heartened that she'd been able to almost joke about it. It looked like she'd be okay with everything after all. Eventually, anyway.

6

Cloudiness

BEFORE GETTING OUT MY HOMEWORK, I sent a quick message to Kyna. Just like last time, she called back almost immediately.

"Excellency, I agree that a meeting such as you suggest is in order. Earlier today I spoke with Lili O'Gara, who also has a few concerns. The Council feels she and her husband may be useful as liaisons going forward, so I will ask them to attend, as well."

"It does make sense to have people already familiar with Jewel from the *Echtran* side do whatever they can to help the newcomers adjust. Maybe the Stuarts should come, too?"

"Certainly," she replied. "Van Stuart is already setting up NuAgra's online systems and Ariel Stuart has offered to mentor the new Healer attached to NuAgra as well. If you'd like, I can suggest all *Echtrans* currently residing in Jewel attend."

"That would be awesome. How soon can we make this happen? And where?"

"The most obvious location is the NuAgra facility itself, Excellency," Kyna replied. "I'll schedule the meeting for tomorrow night, if you can arrange to be there. You don't yet have a driver's license, as I recall?"

"No, I got back to Jewel too late to get into Driver's Ed this semester so I have to wait till spring. The O'Garas can probably drive me, though."

"Very well. I'll message you as soon as a time is set."

Relieved, I flicked off my omni and got started on my homework, confident now that we'd be able to head off any potential problems before they had a chance to spiral out of control.

When Uncle Louie got home a couple of hours later, I was doubly glad I'd requested that meeting.

"Four more sales today," he crowed the moment he walked in the kitchen door. "That's *nine* so far this week and it's only Wednesday!"

He set the two packages he was carrying on the kitchen table and then, amazingly, went over to Aunt Theresa and kissed her on the cheek—something I couldn't remember ever witnessing before.

"Louie!" she admonished him, looking embarrassed—kind of hilarious considering they'd been married for something like thirty years. "That's…very good news, dear," she added when he backed off, still grinning.

"I still can't get over how friendly all these new folks are. A couple of Monday's buyers stopped back in and invited us all to dinner next week—and then the couple I was drawing up papers for did the same thing!"

I could feel Aunt Theresa's surge of alarm. "You didn't accept, did you?"

He stared at her. "Of course I did! I want them to send more customers my way, don't I? The second couple mentioned having two daughters who'll be attending Jewel High with Marsha."

Though my aunt looked slightly reassured, I had no illusions about why these new *Echtrans* were buttering up my uncle.

"I figure we can invite them to our house sometime, too," he continued. "You know, show some Hoosier hospitality. Oh, and one of yesterday's buyers stopped by to drop off a big box of fudge and another couple brought me this, for my family, they said."

Picking up the smaller of the two packages he'd brought in, he handed it to Aunt Theresa. She opened it cautiously, as though she expected it to explode.

"I tried to explain to them that here in Indiana it's the locals who give housewarming gifts to new neighbors, not the other way around, but they insisted."

"Oh, my," Aunt Theresa exclaimed, lifting a beautiful crystal statuette from the box. "This is lovely." But the look she sent me was definitely worried.

I was even more concerned than Aunt Theresa, but tried not to show it. I'd seen that statuette at Glitterby's last week and happened to know it cost a couple hundred dollars. Definitely not okay. Something else to address at tomorrow night's meeting, to nip this sort of thing in the bud.

Meanwhile, Uncle Louie absolutely needed to be clued in so he wouldn't accept any more gifts—bribes?—or invitations.

I said as much to Aunt Theresa when he went upstairs to change out of his work clothes while we got dinner on the table. "We need to tell him," I whispered. "Tonight. Before this kind of thing gets out of hand."

Her brows drew together doubtfully. "Do you really think that's wise? He may be my husband, but I'm by no means blind to his weaknesses. In fact, I know them all too well. He—"

Uncle Louie bounced back into the kitchen, so she broke off.

"I've got a funny story to tell you over dinner." He sat down, grinning at us across his plate of spaghetti. "You know my buddy Greg, our mechanic at the lot? He says when he was leaving

Saturday afternoon those black SUVs from the FBI were behind him for a ways, I guess after they left here. And get this—he swears when he looked in his rear view mirror, he recognized the President—of the United States!—leaning forward from the back seat. Isn't that a hoot?"

Shaking his head, he picked up his fork. "Like the *President* could visit little Jewel, Indiana without it being all over the news? He felt pretty foolish when I told him why those cars were really here. Gave me a good laugh, especially since Greg always accuses *me* of exaggerating. I'm gonna be able to hold this one over his head for a long time."

Still chuckling, he took a big bite of spaghetti, so didn't notice the panicked look Aunt Theresa shot me across the table. For a moment I wondered if it *might* be possible to keep Uncle Louie in the dark indefinitely, he was so incredibly clueless. But it was too risky.

Before he could launch into another story, I cleared my throat. "Um, Uncle Louie, there's something you ought to know."

"Uh-oh. You're not gonna tell me you really are in trouble with the FBI, are you?" he joked.

"Marsha," Aunt Theresa said urgently. "Are you sure—?"

"Whoa." Uncle Louie looked from her to me and back, his smile fading. "What did you do?"

"No, it's nothing like that. I'm not in any trouble. But *you* could stir some up by accident if I don't tell you what's really going on."

"Huh?"

Aunt Theresa surprised me by speaking up first. "Louie, those black cars that were here on Saturday weren't from the FBI. Your friend Greg was right, I'm afraid. The President of the United States *was* here—in our house. The other cars were his Secret Service detail."

"Huh?" Uncle Louie repeated, looking even more confused.

I took over. "He came to thank me for, um, something I did. His visit is why Aunt Theresa had to finally be told the truth about me. And now, with so many of these newcomers trying to get chummy, you need to know, too."

Uncle Louie kept looking back and forth between us. "The President? Really? Here? Uh…what truth?"

I took a deep breath before launching into what I hoped would be a coherent explanation. "About a year ago, I learned about a secret human colony under the surface of the planet Mars. I also learned that's where my parents—my birth parents—came from. In fact, I was born there myself but brought to Earth as a baby before my parents were killed."

I went on to tell him about the monarchy there, how I was heir to the Martian throne, then all the events of the last year, including how I'd gone to Mars and why more and more Martians would be coming to Earth—and Jewel. Uncle Louie didn't say a word the whole time I was talking but his eyes kept getting bigger and bigger.

"Anyway," I concluded, "this new company, NuAgra, is mostly a cover so a bunch of new *Echtrans*—that's what expatriate Martians are called—can move to Jewel without people getting too suspicious."

For nearly a full minute he just sat there, blinking, his eyes again darting back and forth between me and Aunt Theresa, who was watching him with a worried frown. Then, suddenly, he laughed.

"Wow, that was a good one, Marsha! You really had me going for a while there. I remember you always did have a good imagination. You should write novels or something. I bet if you sent that story to a magazine, they'd pay you for it."

Aunt Theresa let out a huff. "I told Marsha you wouldn't believe us, but it's true, Louie. All of it."

His grin faded and he looked at her almost pityingly. "Oh,

come on, Theresa, you don't mean she actually managed to convince *you* of all that stuff? I thought you had more sense than that. Shoot, more sense than me, even."

"Didn't you hear what I said at the start? The *President of the United States* came here, to *our* house. I met him myself, at our own front door. After he left, Lili O'Gara and a woman who'd come here with him sat me down in our living room and told me everything that Marsha just told you. I didn't want to believe it either, but I had no choice."

"But…but…how—?"

"I know it's a lot, Uncle Louie," I said gently. "It took Aunt Theresa a few days before it really sank in. If it'll help, I can prove it."

He looked at me, slightly dazed. "Prove it? How?"

"Just a sec."

I ran upstairs and grabbed my omni off my nightstand, then hurried back down to the kitchen.

"This is probably the easiest way. They call this an omni." I held up the little device, no bigger than a flash drive or a pack of gum. "It's Martian technology, kind of like a smartphone on steroids. Watch." I touched the tiny button on the end.

When the holographic control panel appeared, Uncle Louie's eyes nearly bugged out of his head. Aunt Theresa also gasped, since she hadn't seen it before.

"How—? What—?" Uncle Louie stammered.

"It does all kinds of stuff—way more than I've had time to learn, yet. But here."

I pulled up the communication screen and replayed Kyna's message from Saturday. Her face appeared in midair and my aunt and uncle both started back.

"Excellency, I must warn you that you will shortly have an extremely important visitor—the President of the United States. He should arrive at your home at approximately five o'clock this evening. You may wish to prepare your relatives in some way beforehand." Kyna's face disappeared and the little screen went dark.

"Unfortunately, I didn't think to check my messages until about a minute before the President got here, or I could have given Aunt Theresa some warning. Look, here's something else it can do."

I touched another spot on the control panel. The screen expanded to about twice the size of our TV and began playing a slideshow I'd downloaded before leaving Nuath.

"That's Thiaraway," I told them as the pictures flashed across the big screen. "It's the capital city of Nuath and where I was Acclaimed Sovereign. There, see that?" I paused at the image of a beautiful pink crystalline structure. "That's the Royal Palace. I lived there most of the summer before coming back home."

I let it show a few more pictures of various places around Nuath, then I shut the omni off. "It can also keep me warm if it's cold outside, act as a rain shield, translate any language into any other, all kinds of cool stuff."

Aunt Theresa and Uncle Louie both stared at me, even though Aunt Theresa had known the truth for a few days now. "Is it… dangerous?" She pointed at the omni.

"Of course not. It's not a weapon or anything, just really useful. I can even communicate with Rigel's grandfather on Mars with it, though there's nearly a half-hour lag now, since the planets are moving farther apart from each other."

Uncle Louie sucked in a breath. "It really *is* true? All of it?"

I nodded—cautiously, because he still looked stunned. Then, before I could even get a read on his emotions, a big smile suddenly broke across his face.

"Cool! And you're, like, their queen? Wow, no wonder the Stuarts and the O'Garas have always been so nice to you—and us. Oh, hey, and you dating Jewel High's star quarterback makes a lot more sense now. See, Theresa? There was a good reason all along, while you thought—"

She cleared her throat and he broke off, looking suddenly embarrassed. "Well, anyway," he continued after an awkward pause, "I think it's great. And the President was really here, at our house?"

"He really was. He, um, gave me a medal. Do you want to see that, too?" I was hugely relieved Uncle Louie was taking the news so much better than Aunt Theresa had.

Until his next words.

"Sure! Say, can I maybe borrow it, show it to my buddies at work? Greg will crow when he finds out he was right all along, but Tom will—"

"No!" Aunt Theresa and I both exclaimed at the same time.

"Uncle Louie, this has to be kept really, *really* secret," I insisted, using all the Royal "push" I could summon. "You can't tell *anybody*. Seriously. Promise you won't?"

His face fell slightly. "Aw, not even Tom? He thinks he's such a big shot, just because his cousin is a councilman up in Chicago. This is so much—"

"Not *anybody*," I repeated, holding his pleading gaze with my own stern one, not giving an inch. "If people in Jewel knew about this, they'd flip out! They'd treat me...all of us...like freaks. And if they got scared, they might even do something bad to me and the others. We have to keep this super, *super* secret. Please, Uncle Louie, you have to promise!"

Now his eyes slid away from mine. "Okay, okay, fine," he mumbled.

I kept watching him for a long moment, thoroughly probing his emotions to tell if he meant it. He seemed to, though grudgingly. Still, I was fairly confident that once he really thought things through he'd keep that promise, no matter how much he was dying to impress his friends.

"Our spaghetti is stone cold," my aunt suddenly said. "I'll have to reheat everything in the microwave. Louie, any other questions you have for Marsha can wait until after she's eaten."

Of course, he still asked a few during dinner, despite Aunt Theresa's frowns. Between answers—and bites of spaghetti—I reminded him several more times how important it was to keep this information to himself. Though he nodded each time, I worried he still didn't completely get it.

"Hey, how about some of that fudge for dessert?" he suggested as Aunt Theresa stacked our empty plates.

I shook my head. "Cormac, my Bodyguard, would go ballistic if I ate something a Martian stranger gave you without letting him taste it first."

"Huh? You mean all these new NuAgra people already know I'm your uncle? Is that why they're buying cars from me and inviting us all to dinner and stuff?"

"Well…yeah. That's the reason I had to tell you all this—so you'd know not to accept any more gifts or invitations from them."

He looked disappointed. "But…how come? Where's the harm?"

"It's just… I don't want them using you—or Aunt Theresa—to get to me. To try to influence me or anything."

My aunt turned from the sink in obvious alarm, soapsuds dripping from her hands. "Didn't you say they weren't dangerous?"

"They're not." At least I had no reason—yet—to think any of them were. "But that's not the point. You guys don't really want to get sucked into *Echtran* politics, do you?"

Aunt Theresa shook her head, looking alarmed, but Uncle Louie shrugged. "Sounds pretty interesting to me," he said. "Seems like there should be *some* perks for the people who took care of their leader all these years."

"Louie!" Aunt Theresa snapped. "Think what you're saying. You're already selling more cars than you ever have, because of... all this. Isn't that enough?"

He sighed. "I guess. I just thought maybe—"

"I'm sorry, but both of those gifts will have to be returned, Uncle Louie. And if you're offered any other presents or invitations, please don't accept. Okay?" Not that there should be any more after tomorrow night's meeting. I planned to make sure of that.

Though obviously disappointed, he reluctantly agreed—then continued to bombard me with questions.

7

Fractures

RIGEL GREETED me with a quick kiss when I got off the bus the next morning—an excellent start to a day that promised to be both interesting and challenging.

"Have you met any of them yet?" I asked as we headed into the school, hand in hand. "None were on my bus this morning."

"Two on mine, the same ones we're supposed to interview. There they are, just ahead of us—Liam and Lucas. Twins, I think." He nodded toward two dark-haired boys, both maybe a hair taller than Rigel though nowhere near as tall as Sean.

"Do they seem nice?"

Rigel shrugged. "We didn't say much more than hi and exchange names, since everyone else on the bus wanted to meet them, too. None of us could exactly let on we had any *special* reason to talk, you know?"

"Right, of course. I wonder—?"

I broke off, sensing someone else's *brath* behind us. Turning discreetly, I saw two girls heading toward us—one around our age, with dark auburn hair, the other one blonde and noticeably younger. Both definitely Martian.

As they drew level with us, I took a half-step forward and smiled. "Hey, welcome to Jewel. I'm Marsha Truitt, but most people call me M. And this is Rigel Stuart."

The younger girl's eyes went wide and she started to stammer something, but the older one—her big sister?—nudged her sharply with an elbow.

"Nice to meet you." She spoke without stammering at all. "And thanks. I'm Kira Morain and this is my sister, Adina."

Unlike her little sister, Kira displayed no nervousness whatsoever, nor did I sense much from her. I was glad. I'd been worried the new kids might act all intimidated and weird around me. This one definitely didn't. In fact, I had the distinct impression she didn't like Rigel or me very much. I could make a pretty good guess why.

"I hope you'll both like it here," he said. "Let us know if we can help with anything while you're still, y'know, getting used to the place."

"I'm sure we'll be fine," Kira replied with only a hint of an answering smile. "But thanks anyway."

They continued on down the hallway while Rigel and I both stared after them.

"Not very friendly, are they?" Rigel said. Then, silently, *What did you sense off them? Did you remember to try?*

I nodded. "Nothing I'd quite call hostile. Adina was mostly just nervous, but Kira… I'm guessing she bought into the gossip in that stupid article. Definitely no warm fuzzies there."

"You'll win her over. All she has to do is get to know you."

His confidence was heartening, but I was more concerned about slurs—or worse—aimed Rigel's way.

"Guess we'll find out, huh? Oops, here comes another one," I added, detecting another distinctly Martian vibe nearby.

This one was a boy, an inch or two shorter than Rigel, with brownish-blond hair. We again made a point of introducing ourselves—casually, for the benefit of any *Duchas* students within earshot.

The boy stopped in his tracks, exuding nearly as much nervousness as little Adina had. "Oh, um, hi. G-Grady. Quinlan. They told me about— But I wasn't—"

"Hey, it's okay." Rigel cut him off before he could blurt out anything he shouldn't. "I know exactly what it's like to be the new kid, trust me. At least you're not the only one this week. That'll help. What year are you in?"

"T-Tenth. Um, sophomore. At least—"

"Do you know what classes you'll have?" I asked before he could yammer on about the special placement tests he'd taken during his orientation training—not something most transfers would have done.

Gulping visibly, he nodded and fumblingly pulled a piece of paper from his pocket. "Um, yeah. It's all right here." Apparently too nervous to read them off, he just handed it to me.

With an inward sigh, I scanned his class list. "I've had most of these teachers. You'll like them, I think. Hope you have a great first day here, Grady." I handed back his course list with a big smile.

He blinked three or four times, turning bright red, then nodded convulsively. "Th-Thanks."

The warning bell rang. He flinched, then hurried off at a near run.

"Definitely nothing hostile there, either," I told Rigel before he could ask. "Poor guy. Guess we'd better get to class."

One of the tall, dark-haired twins Rigel had pointed out was already talking with Molly when we reached Pre-Cal. She motioned us over as soon as she spotted us.

"Have you guys met Liam yet?"

"We met on the bus." Rigel extended his hand. "Guess they didn't want to put you and your brother in all the same classes?"

Liam shrugged. "Nah, Lucas tested into AP Calc. He's way more into math and science than I am. So, Rigel, I didn't get a chance on the bus to ask you all the football stuff I want to know…the, um, season so far, I mean," he added, apparently realizing how odd it would sound to a *Duchas* that he didn't know much about the sport itself, yet.

"Yeah, sure, maybe we can talk at lunch," Rigel agreed with a grin that acknowledged Liam's near-slip.

Deb joined us then, also eager to be introduced, so we stuck to strictly non-Martian topics until class started.

Kira was in my French class next period, but seemed no more eager to chat than before. Finally, as we were leaving class, Molly got her talking a little—enough to find out she was a senior, like Sean, and that her family had moved into the Diamond View Terrace Apartments.

"Then you should be riding our same bus," Molly said with a quick smile that Kira didn't echo. "Or do you drive to school?"

Kira shook her head. "We just have the one car. Our dad dropped us off today but next week, well…see ya." She headed off down the hall without a backward glance.

Molly frowned after her. "Not very friendly, is she?" she said, just like Rigel had. "She's probably just nervous. I'm sure she'll warm up to us once she gets used to everything."

But I knew nervousness had nothing to do with it. Interesting that her parents had apparently been among those sucking up to Uncle Louie while Kira clearly wanted nothing to do with me. I wondered what was really going on there.

The only other new *Echtran* I met before lunchtime was Liam's brother Lucas, since they were both in my next two classes. Lucas was quieter than his brother but not noticeably more nervous around me. As they walked with Rigel and me from Chemistry to English Lit, Lucas turned to us both with a tentative smile.

"Do, um, you think we can all get together sometime soon and talk?" He spoke quietly enough that no nearby non-Martians were likely to hear him. "I read all the reports from last week but they were kind of sketchy. There's a whole lot more I'd really like to know about…what happened."

"Sure," I replied. "If not today, maybe tomorrow. You know about the, um, meeting tonight, right? I'll be answering questions there, too."

At lunch, I was briefly alarmed to see all the new students sitting together. Then I realized that would be perfectly normal even if they weren't *Echtrans*, since they'd supposedly all moved here from "back East."

Not suprisingly, their table was already mobbed by people eager to meet them. Trina and her "welcoming committee" were doing their best to monopolize their attention but they weren't the only ones, by a long shot. Discreetly resting my arm against Rigel's while we ate, I listened in on some of the conversations.

I didn't like everything I heard.

"So, my dad wanted me to ask you guys if NuAgra is going to start hiring locally anytime soon?" Nate Villiers was saying to the group.

One of the *Echtrans* I hadn't met yet, a tall, blond guy, answered. "I don't think they've decided yet, sorry. They probably want to get all their own people situated first."

I relaxed slightly. It sounded like he'd been well-coached, which probably meant the others had, too.

"Yeah, well, there are a lot of people around here who could use the work, you know? Maybe mention that to somebody there?" Nate persisted. He'd apparently had some coaching, too, making me wonder what his father did—and if he was currently out of work.

Nor was Nate the only one to ask that question. Understandable, given how many automotive-related jobs we'd lost over the past few years, but still awkward. I hoped it wouldn't lead to widespread resentment against the newcomers.

Don't borrow trouble, okay? Rigel thought, picking up on my worry. *Even if NuAgra can't hire Duchas, they'll still prop up the local economy. That'll help a lot.*

Hope so. Uncle Louie's been saying that, too, even before I told him the truth about them.

I'd given Rigel the rundown on that conversation when I went to bed last night. Even more than the convenience of our new long-distance telepathy, I loved the feeling of falling asleep in each other's thoughts.

Me, too, Rigel thought to me now, with a grin that made my heart speed up. *Probably my favorite thing about our new range.*

Toward the end of lunch, when the regular Jewel students had finally dispersed to their own tables to eat, we discovered the locals weren't the only ones grumbling.

"They seriously want us to act like these *Duchas*?" the tall blond guy said softly to the others. "That's going to be harder than I thought."

"At least *you* only have to fake it until next May, Alan," said the young-looking dark-haired girl sitting next to Adina. "I've got three more years after this one!" Jana, the other freshman, then.

Liam and Lucas exchanged glances, then Liam shrugged. "At least we'll have an edge getting onto any sports teams we want. Sounds like Rigel Stuart and Sean O'Gara became stars, like, instantly, and they're not—"

Abruptly, Rigel moved his arm away from mine so we couldn't hear any more.

Sorry, he thought to me. *That was starting to get weird.*

I raised an eyebrow at him. *If there's trouble brewing on the* Echtran *side, too, we need to know.*

He gave a tiny nod. *Yeah, you're right. Can't afford to be squeamish.* He shifted his arm back to graze mine and immediately we could hear them perfectly again.

"—seems like a nice enough guy," Lucas was saying to the others. "Whatever the real story is between him and the Sovereign, I can't believe he's a Faxon sympathizer."

Rigel flinched but didn't pull his arm away.

"Maybe not," Alan said, "but he's still way crossing the line. Look at him, sitting right next to her over there. You'd think O'Gara would have something to say about it, wouldn't you? I used to play *chas pell*, um, basketball with him when we were kids, before his family left Nuath. He didn't seem like the type who'd just roll over without a fight."

All three of the younger girls looked over to where Sean was again sitting with some basketball teammates.

"Yeah, poor Sean." Jana, the freshman who'd been complaining before, sighed. "Maybe one of us should console him, you think?"

The warning bell rang, putting a stop to our eavesdropping—to Rigel's obvious relief.

"Really not a fan of that," he murmured to me as we rose to return our trays. "Seems underhanded, you know?"

"More than me using that emotion-sensing thing no one else knows about?" I was careful to use our secret sub-whisper.

"That's different. More like…being super-good at reading body language. And it's not like our lives or even our safety's on the line here."

"You can't know that," I retorted. *But if it bothers you that much, we won't do it again,* I finished silently. *Unless we have a really good reason.*

Deal.

Still, after what we'd overheard Alan saying, I mentally added that topic to my agenda for tonight's meeting. Rigel might not be in favor of another MARSTAR bulletin but I could at least try to make sure he didn't have to deal with any more backbiting here at school.

When I got home from school, I set right to work on my opening speech for tonight and had a decent draft written by the time Aunt Theresa got home. She looked worried again.

"Is something wrong?" I asked, just like I had yesterday.

"I'm not sure. I hope not. But your uncle just texted me that he'd be late for dinner because he and some coworkers are stopping by Green's after work to celebrate their good sales week."

She always got ticked off when Uncle Louie went out drinking with his friends but what I sensed from her was more than that.

"You don't think he'll say anything to them, do you? About…you know."

"I'd *like* to think he has a bit more sense than that, but I know how he loves to spin stories to impress his friends, especially after a beer or two. I can't help worrying he might get carried away."

"I'm sure he won't." I tried to sound more confident than I felt.

"You're probably right. At any rate, we won't wait dinner on him. Especially as you have that NuAgra thing tonight. Did you put the roast into the oven when you got home?"

I nodded. "I saw your note on the fridge. But that reminds me, I should check to make sure they haven't changed the time of the meeting."

Hurrying up to my room, I went to my nightstand…but the omni wasn't there. I was almost sure I'd left it right next to my alarm clock.

"Huh," I said out loud, pulling open the drawer. Had I stuck it back into my old glasses case out of habit? Nope. Not there, either.

After a quick search of my whole nightstand, then the floor and bed next to it, I went back downstairs.

"Aunt Theresa, I didn't leave my omni down here last night after showing it to you and Uncle Louie, did I?"

She turned from the sink, where she was scrubbing potatoes, to blink at me in surprise. "Not that I noticed. And I believe I would have noticed."

"Weird. I couldn't find it in my room. I'll go look again."

I went back up and checked all my drawers and even emptied out my backpack, since once or twice during last week's Grentl crisis I'd brought it to school with me. Nothing. Then a terrible suspicion entered my mind. Surely, *surely* Uncle Louie wouldn't have taken it?

He had said something about wanting to show my Medal of Freedom to his buddies, but Aunt Theresa and I had quickly totally vetoed that—and the medal was still on my dresser. He *had* to know waving my omni around would be even worse. Didn't he?

Hoping like crazy I was wrong, I headed back down to the kitchen. Not wanting to scare Aunt Theresa—yet—I didn't say anything, just helped her cut up the veggies to add to the pot roast for its last hour in the oven. After that I did my best to concentrate on the last bit of my speech and then on some home-work, but I couldn't help worrying. And searching my room again.

We'd already finished eating when Uncle Louie walked in.

"Finally!" my aunt huffed at him. "You'll have to reheat your dinner in the microwave, as it's cold by now."

"Oops, sorry. Guess it's later than I thought."

It was obvious he'd been drinking, and probably more than the two beers Aunt Theresa always insisted had to be his limit.

Since the O'Garas would be here any minute to pick me up, I didn't have time to beat around the bush.

"Hi, Uncle Louie," I said brightly. "You didn't happen to do something with my omni, did you? I can't seem to find it." I quickly focused in case he lied to me.

He didn't. "Oh, um, yeah, sorry. I, er, saw it lying on the table and figured that wasn't a good place for it, so I kind of, um stuck it in my pocket. Sorry. Here." Looking slightly embarrassed, he fished it out of his pants pocket and handed it to me.

Aunt Theresa dropped the pan she was rinsing into the sink with a clatter. "Louie! You took that with you to work? To that bar? What if someone had seen it? What would you have told them?"

"Don't worry, Theresa, I couldn't make it do anything." He seemed more disgruntled than apologetic.

"You mean you tried?" I demanded.

He shrugged. "Maybe just a little. It was so cool, what you showed us last night..." He trailed off, both of our horrified expressions finally registering. "Sorry," he repeated, more sincerely this time.

"I thought you understood how important—" I began, then heard the O'Garas' car pulling into our driveway. "I've got to go. But Uncle Louie, you *can't* do anything like this again. Seriously!"

Shamefaced now, he nodded. "I know. I won't."

He seemed to really mean it this time but I'd make absolutely sure of that when I got back. "Okay. I'll try not to be too late tonight, Aunt Theresa. Bye!"

As I left the kitchen I saw her turning the same expression on Uncle Louie she'd turned on me more times than I could count.

Nope, he definitely hadn't heard the last about how foolish he'd been. Nobody could lecture like my aunt. Maybe I wouldn't need to say much to him myself after all.

8

Crystallization

IT HAD BEEN at least six months since I'd been past the old transmission plant on the outskirts of Jewel. As the O'Garas' car approached it now, I was stunned by how dramatically it had changed.

The four enormous metal buildings were still there, but instead of squatting in an endless expanse of trash-strewn dirt and weeds, they were now surrounded by lush green grass dotted with young trees. Newly-planted shrubs and flowers bordered a long drive leading to the freshly-painted complex. A large green sign by the gate read, "NuAgra—Nu Crops for a New World."

Mr. O'Gara slowed the minivan to a halt in front of an imposing looking steel gate set in an equally imposing ten-foot fence that stretched in both directions. Cormac, who'd followed in his own car, pulled up behind us.

A man stepped out of the small guard house next to the gate as Mr. O lowered his window.

"Quinn and Lili O'Gara, our children Sean and Molly, and

Sovereign Emileia," he informed the guard, who took a quick step backward, then bowed deeply.

"We are honored. Please proceed."

The huge gates silently swung open and Mr. O drove forward, up a long, white-graveled drive.

"Wow." I gazed around at the impressively manicured grounds. "How did they manage all of this so fast?"

"Nearly half of Jewel's new *Echtrans* are from the Agricultural *fine*," Mrs. O'Gara replied. "Though they originally acquired the sod and plants from a commercial landscaping company, their abilities allowed them to achieve this effect far more quickly than would have been possible otherwise."

"What you see out here is merely cosmetic, of course," Mr. O added, "though I understand some important agricultural research has already begun in the greenhouses and fields behind the facility."

That seemed incredible, considering most of the researchers had arrived less than a week ago. We pulled into the big parking area near the central building, which displayed the same NuAgra logo and slogan I'd seen on the fence.

"They've done a good job making it look legit," Sean commented as we walked up to the main entrance. "Like any other *Duchas* R&D facility."

Or not. Mr. O stepped up to a small panel just outside the glass doors and placed his palm on it. "No non-*Echtran* will be allowed inside, for obvious reasons."

"Won't that seem kind of…suspicious?" I asked.

"Not really," Mrs. O assured me. "Many companies have stringent security in place to prevent corporate espionage. We've made no secret of the fact that some of the research here will be of a sensitive nature, so our protocols should seem perfectly reasonable."

Once we'd each had our palms read by the little screen, the glass doors opened as silently as the outer gate had done.

Stepping through, I had a moment of unpleasant *deja vu*—the decor, with its soothingly blue walls and soft lighting, was disturbingly reminiscent of the Mind Healing facility on Nuath. The place Rigel's memory had been erased.

That familiarity faded when Mr. O led us down a short hallway, around a corner, then into a large room laid out like a lecture hall. Ranks of tables, nearly half of them already full, sloped up from a central podium. I entered near the podium and everyone immediately rose to their feet and bowed, right fists over hearts.

I made the proper inclination of my head, surreptitiously scanning the big room for Rigel. He'd said he'd be here, but what if—? I spotted him then, along with his parents, among those still filtering in through double doors at the upper end of the room. Brightening, I sent a quick, silent greeting.

Mom's shift at the hospital ran a little late, he explained. *Glad we made it before things got started.*

The prevailing mood in the room had felt positive when I first entered, but as the Stuarts moved down the center aisle to take the seats reserved for them in the front row, I sensed a distinct change. Focusing first on one, then another, I picked up resentment, distaste, curiosity and, in a few cases, outrage. With an effort I smoothed my instinctive frown, determined not to let my worry show.

It's fine, M. They just need time to get used to the idea, that's all.

I wasn't as confident but this was no time to argue. Already, Mr. O'Gara was stepping up to the podium, clearly in his element —which was another unpleasant reminder of my time in Nuath, this time recalling how close I'd come to appointing him Regent before discovering his duplicity about Rigel. He'd earned back some of my trust since then, but not all of it.

Gazing up at the assembly, he cleared his throat, then waited while the murmuring that had begun at the Stuarts' entrance subsided. "Fellow *Echtrans*, I give you Sovereign Emileia."

Now cheers broke out, along with a few shouts of *Faoda byo Thiarna Emileia!* (long live Sovereign Emileia). Mr. O stepped down to join his family and the Stuarts in the front row and I moved to the podium. The earlier negativity I'd sensed had dissipated, which unfortunately only confirmed it had been directed at Rigel.

"Thank you, everyone, for coming tonight on such short notice," I began.

When nervousness briefly threatened, I quickly recalled all the speeches I'd made back on Mars—usually to far less receptive crowds. It helped. Straightening my shoulders, I continued.

"I'd like to take this opportunity to welcome you all to Jewel, Indiana, and to salute the courage you've demonstrated by leaving your homes and all that was familiar for the good of Nuath. Though I know Jewel is not what you've been used to, I'm sure in time you will grow to love it as I do.

"Each of you was specially chosen to come here as representing the most dedicated and trustworthy of our newest arrivals. For myself, I'm deeply honored that so many of you requested to live in the town I call home. While the people here are not as sophisticated or technologically advanced as we are, they do have valuable qualities of their own that I hope you will learn to appreciate as you get to know them better.

"The good people of Jewel are understandably curious about NuAgra, and you, so don't be surprised when your new neighbors begin asking questions. Never forget, however, that it's imperative you raise no suspicions about our true origins. I understand you've each been given complete life histories, which should help to avoid that.

"Already there is some speculation in Jewel about NuAgra's hiring plans as well as concern that it could pose unwelcome competition to certain businesses. We'll need to work together to soothe any resentment or worries along those lines without revealing too much. Going out of your way to be friendly and continuing to patronize local merchants should help the towns-people to realize that NuAgra and its people will be positive additions to their community.

"I should give those of you attending Jewel High fair warning that our school newspaper plans to do stories on each of you, so be thinking about how you might answer interview questions."

The students in the room started exchanging nervous looks so I added, "If you have questions about what to say, I'll be happy to answer them tonight or tomorrow at school. Or you can ask Sean or Molly O'Gara, or Rigel Stuart."

I again sensed quick spurts of hostility from around the big room at the mention of Rigel's name. That stiffened my resolve to deliver the less conciliating part of my speech, though Rigel had firmly vetoed the part I'd wanted to add about him.

"As you settle in, please feel free to reach out to the O'Garas, the Stuarts, our local *Echtran* Council members, or to me through them, with any questions or issues you might have. However, I must ask that you *not* approach me by way of my adoptive aunt or uncle or any of my non-*Echtran* friends. While I appreciate the thought behind them, surely you must understand that gifts and dinner invitations extended to my uncle at work are completely inappropriate and cannot be accepted."

A couple in the second row shifted uncomfortably in their seats, radiating guilt. The Morains, I guessed, since they were sitting with Kira and Adina. A few scattered others exhibited varying degrees of surprise, resentment and irritation, though I didn't pause long enough to pinpoint exactly who felt what.

"I'm sure many of you have questions, so I'd like to invite Mr. and Mrs. O'Gara and Dr. and Mr. Stuart to join me down front to help address them. Again, thank you very much for coming."

Before the O'Garas or Stuarts could even leave their seats, several hands went up.

"Yes?" I pointed to the woman who'd raised her hand first.

She stood up. "Excellency, is it true that you and Rigel Stuart have actually begun dating again?"

See? I thought to Rigel, who was still seated. *I was afraid of this.*

"Yes, it's true, though that wasn't the sort of question I had in mind."

Half a dozen more hands shot into the air. I nodded toward a thin, black-haired man.

"Yes?"

"Does he really have his memory back? Or was it never actually erased at all?"

I sighed inwardly. "Yes, he has his memory back, and yes, it really was erased—the last year of it, anyway."

"But I thought he promised to stay away from you, for the good of our people," a woman near the back blurted out without waiting to be called on. "Back on Nuath we were told—"

"I know what you were told," I snapped before she could say anything really nasty. "But Rigel Stuart—"

M! Don't! Rigel's urgent thought stopped me in mid-sentence. *Don't say anything we'll both end up regretting. Please!"*

Taking a deep breath, I forced myself to calm down. He was right that lashing out in anger was likely to do more harm than good.

"—is not the topic we're here to discuss," I finished. "The Council plans to issue another statement soon, addressing that particular situation. Meanwhile, we'll be happy to address any questions you have about *Jewel*—the community, ways to get involved locally, that sort of thing."

Most of the other hands slowly went down. Apparently their owners had *all* wanted to ask questions about Rigel and me. I pointed at one of the few who still had a hand up. "Yes?"

"Will we be able to have any social activities just for…us?" a blonde woman asked. "Or will that look too suspicious?"

Dr. Stuart took that one, probably realizing I needed more time to compose myself. "As long as it's presented as a NuAgra function, something like that should be fine," she said with a smile. "But if Jewel is to be our permanent home, we mustn't limit all of our socializing to other *Echtrans*. As the Sovereign said, it's important that we be seen as contributing members of this community. We mustn't appear stand-offish, or the towns-people might assume we consider ourselves better than they are."

A nervous chuckle went through the room.

"Yes, I know that in many ways we *are* superior," she continued. "But if we make our neighbors feel inferior, they're bound to resent that. Wouldn't you?"

There was some shrugging and nodding. At least some of them seemed to get it.

"More questions?" Mr. O'Gara asked then. "Yes?"

"Will we have a secure way to send messages to our friends and family back in Nuath any time soon?"

Mr. Stuart fielded that one, describing the system he was already putting in place for exactly that purpose. Now sticking to more appropriate topics, the Q&A went on for another hour before Mr. O finally called a halt.

"I believe that will do for tonight, as it's either a work night or a school night for most of us. Further questions can be directed to me or to any other *Echtrans* who have resided in Jewel for a while."

Stepping back up to the podium, I said, "I hope to have more forums like this going forward. Perhaps monthly, if that proves convenient. Once more, thank you all for coming. Good night."

The moment I stepped down, several dozen people surged forward, clearly eager to speak privately with me. The first to reach me were the Morains, who both bowed deeply. I now vaguely remembered meeting the tall, red-haired man and willowy blonde woman before—either on Nuath or when making my last-minute stops at the few *Echtran* compounds in the U.S. before returning to Jewel last month.

"Excellency, please allow us to apologize!" the woman exclaimed, radiating distress as she straightened. "You were right, of course, that inviting you to dinner through your uncle was inappropriate. But when Mona and Brad came up while we—"

She broke off, looking stricken. "Oh! I'm so sorry, Excellency! I should have introduced myself at once. I'm Deirdra Morain and this is my husband, Aidan. And these—"

She turned to her daughters who were hanging back—Kira with a slightly disgusted look on her face, probably because of the way her mother was abasing herself to me. I couldn't blame her.

"Yes, I remember you, Deirdra. Didn't you tell me in Dun Cloch you'd been acquainted with my mother? And I met Kira and Adina at school this morning," I added before she could drag them forward. "It's all right, really. You hadn't been warned yet."

"Still, we should have known better," Aidan said, looking nearly as abashed as his wife. He reminded me slightly of Mr. O, who now stepped forward.

Extending his hand, he said, "Quinn O'Gara. Please, don't worry about this. As you'll learn, our Sovereign rarely stands on ceremony. We will likely discover other areas that should have been addressed in advance of everyone's arrival, but no one will be held responsible for acting in ignorance."

"Thank you. Thank you both!" With another deep bow, the Morain family moved off.

Others moved up, eager to introduce themselves. The Galloways and the Vaughns, who'd given Uncle Louie the fudge and the figurine, offered apologies nearly as abject as the Morains had.

I did my best to be gracious but Cormac, who'd stood silently throughout my speech and the questions, now marred his usual impassivity by glowering as he returned their gifts to them. As I'd predicted, he'd been particularly alarmed by the fudge.

Rigel hung back at first so I could get a read on those who came up without any hostility they might feel toward him complicating their emotions. Mostly I just detected excitement and nervousness at meeting the Sovereign—until Rigel moved closer. Then, though no one had the nerve to say anything rude to him in front of me, the feelings I sensed turned distinctly darker. Not good.

"You'll have plenty of opportunities in the future to speak with the Sovereign," Mr. O finally said to the small crowd still waiting, "but it's time we took her home."

I didn't argue, since all this emotion-reading was tiring. "Have a nice evening, everyone. Good night."

Not until I was leaving did it occur to me that the people I should have been trying to read were the ones who *didn't* want to come up and meet me. Oh, well. As Mr. O said, there'd be plenty of time for that later.

Hanging back for a moment as we left the building, I took Rigel's hand. Several people—including the O'Garas—frowned at that, but I didn't much care. I needed the recharging I always got from him and I also wanted to get a better read on *his* feelings. Not surprisingly, they were conflicted.

What was that bit about a statement from the Council? he silently asked as we crossed the parking lot a few steps behind his parents. *I thought we'd agreed—*

I know, but something *has to be done. I can't just stand there and smile while people bad-mouth you. You know you couldn't, if it were me they were dissing.*

Maybe that's true, but—

I promise not to say anything that's likely to scare people or make them want to separate us, but they all need to understand—

I broke off. Another couple had angled toward the Stuarts just ahead of us. Prompted by their expressions, I quickly focused on their emotions. Definitely hostile.

"You should be ashamed," the woman hissed to Dr. Stuart, so softly that I never would have heard her if I hadn't been holding Rigel's hand. "Since you clearly can't control your son, you should never have brought him back to Jewel."

"My wife is right," said the man, more loudly. "What you are allowing is little short of treason. Your whole family is a disgrace to your *fine* and to the Martian race."

They noticed me watching then and quickly moved off. Rigel started after them, glowering, but his mother put a hand on his arm when he would have brushed past her.

"No, Rigel. Let it go. It's only words. Anything you do or say will only make things worse."

"People are still unsettled." Mr. Stuart's calming tone belied his own anger and worry. "It's been an emotional few days for them all. Give them some time."

Rigel, still furious, just glared after the couple. Not until we'd separated, him to go with his parents to their car and me to go with the O'Garas, did he finally send me a silent, angry message.

You're right. We need to do something. It's one thing for people to say stuff about me, but when they insult my mom to her face—

I do have an idea, I thought back. *Let me play with it a little tonight and I'll run it past you tomorrow. Love you!*

9

Dispersion

I GREETED Rigel at my locker before school the next morning with a kiss and a grin.

"What?" he asked suspiciously. "You seem pretty pleased with yourself. I tried to ask on the way to school—"

"Sorry, I wanted to actually show you what I came up with rather than try to tell you long-distance. Here." I dug a sheet of paper out of my backpack and handed it to him to read.

"It was me blurting out that the Council would send the statement that gave me the idea," I explained as he scanned it. "They asked me to write it, but they didn't say it had to come *from* me, even if that's what they had in mind. What do you think?"

Slowly, he nodded. "This just might work. I hadn't thought about doing it like this."

It's just a draft, I thought to him as we headed to class, *but if we can polish it up by the end of the day, I'll send it to Kyna. She seemed pretty ticked about how the Council handled the first statement, so with any luck she won't feel like she has to run this past them before sending it out over MARSTAR.*

At lunch, we both grabbed sandwiches and went to the court-yard again. Getting this statement out was my top priority now, and the new *Echtran* students could always catch me between classes or at tonight's football game if they had questions.

"Hope the new kids will be okay with those interviews now," Rigel murmured as he and I walked hand in hand to the buses after Publications, where Angela had been urging everyone to get cracking.

"They've been well coached, so I doubt there'll be any slip-ups. To be honest, I'm more worried about my Uncle Louie. He's obviously dying to tell his buddies about his niece the Martian Princess."

Rigel's brows drew down. "He wouldn't, would he?"

"Not after the lecture he got last night from Aunt Theresa. I just hope he didn't say anything dumb while he was at Green's last night—with my omni in his pocket."

"He took your omni?" Rigel's concern spiked to alarm. "What if he—"

"Don't worry. Its security settings are so high nobody but me can make it work. If he did show it to his friends, they probably thought it was just a futuristic-looking flash drive. Judging by his mood when he got home last night, the worst that happened was he got laughed at."

Rigel squeezed my hand. "I hope you're right. The last thing we need is—" He broke off as we moved into the crowd around the buses and finished silently, *townspeople worrying about some alien invasion, with you at the head of it!*

And you accuse me *of borrowing trouble?*

You're right. Smiling, he leaned in for a quick kiss. "See you at the game tonight?"

"Wouldn't miss it." I returned his kiss as wholeheartedly as I dared, with so many people around. Still smiling, I boarded my bus.

As usual for a Friday during football season, most of the conversation was about tonight's game—and Rigel. Bri was already mapping out the plays she thought our guys should run. Deb, Molly and I indulged her, exchanging occasional amused glances at her obsessiveness.

"I'm giving you a ride again, right?" Deb asked when she and Bri were about to get off at their stop.

"Yep, unless I call and say otherwise. I forgot to ask if Rigel's folks are driving me home after, but I can let you know once we're there."

Bri turned quickly. "You guys should both come to the after-party tonight. I'm sure there'll be one."

Before I could argue, someone complained that she was holding things up so she hurried off the bus with a wave.

"She never gives up, does she?" Molly murmured as the bus started moving again. "Think your aunt might actually let you go, now that she knows?"

I shrugged. "I probably shouldn't use it for that kind of leverage, but...maybe I'll ask."

Once I got home, I dictated the final version of my statement into my omni, then sent it to Kyna with a request that it go out as soon as possible. I half expected to hear back from her right away, like the last two times, but she still hadn't responded when Aunt Theresa got home an hour later.

"Is something wrong, Aunt Theresa?" She looked even more worried than she had the past two afternoons.

This time, she nodded. "I'm afraid so. After you left for school this morning, Louie admitted he'd told a few of his friends about you last night—about the whole, ah, Martian situation. He *claims* nobody believed him, that they just laughed when he couldn't get that gadget of yours to do anything, but what if he's wrong?"

Obviously my instincts had been spot-on. Unfortunately. "They probably did just laugh. Without any proof, it had to sound like a totally crazy story." I tried hard to convince myself along with her. Because if just one person had taken him seriously…

The phone rang, making both of us jump before Aunt Theresa moved to answer it. "Hello?"

Still edgy, I shamelessly eavesdropped.

"Mrs. Truitt?" came a male voice from the other end. "This is Ted from Bulls-Eye Whitetail Ranch and Specialty Meats. Like some of the other local merchants, we'd like to honor this year's Jewel High Homecoming Court. Your niece was this year's Junior Princess, right?"

Aunt Theresa glanced at me, relaxed and smiling now. I tried to look clueless, since I hadn't told her about my super-sensitive Martian hearing. "Yes. Yes, she was."

"Great! We're giving each member of the Court five pounds of venison steaks and sausage, with our compliments. If she can arrange to come out here around six o'clock, we'd also like to get a promotional photo."

"Oh. Certainly. Thank you very much." Still smiling, she hung up the phone, then repeated everything she'd just been told.

I felt strangely reluctant, even though I'd been doing this sort of thing all week.

"Six o'clock? That's right when Deb was supposed to be picking me up for the game. And there's no way Rigel or the cheerleaders on the Court can be there, since they have to get there early."

"I imagine they're taking individual pictures, like the antique store. In any event, I said you'd be there—and venison isn't easy to come by these days. You know how your Uncle Louie loves it."

"But—"

Now she frowned. "Marsha, I realize Junior Class Homecoming Princess doesn't compare to…all those other important things you've been doing, but it *is* the only honor I'm allowed to tell my friends about."

Remembering her near-slip during the electronics store photo shoot, I realized it must be nearly as hard for her to resist boasting about her niece, the Martian ruler who'd saved the world, as it was for Uncle Louie. She just had more self-control.

"Okay. Do you know where this place is?"

Her smile broadened. "Of course. I'll drive you, then take you on to the game afterward, as the ranch is along the way. I don't particularly like you riding with one of your young friends who's had her license for such a short time, anyway. I'd think your, ah, people wouldn't care for that, either."

"Yeah, probably not. I'll let Deb know."

Though the timing still seemed weird to me, I phoned Deb, then went upstairs to change into something picture-worthy. For Aunt Theresa's sake I'd play along—though I hoped it wouldn't make me late to the game.

———

The deer hunting ranch was about three miles northeast of Jewel High, where corn and soybean fields gave way to several hundred acres of woods. At the Bulls-Eye sign, Aunt Theresa turned up a long, winding drive that gradually changed from pavement to gravel to dirt.

At two minutes till six, we pulled up in front of a building marked "Specialty Meats and Hunting Supplies." There was a battered pickup truck off to one side, but no other cars were in the front lot. In fact, the store looked like it was already closed.

"Are we too late?" I asked, secretly relieved.

Aunt Theresa got out and walked to the door to peer through the glass top. "He said six o'clock—and I see someone moving around." She pushed on the door and it opened. "Hello?"

As I joined her, a burly man emerged from behind a counter at the back of the store. Though I'd definitely never been here before, he looked vaguely familiar. Maybe I'd seen him in town.

"Miz Truitt," he exclaimed, looking surprised but not particularly pleased. "I…didn't know you planned to come out as well."

"I'm afraid Marsha doesn't drive yet," my aunt explained, moving forward. "I'll be dropping her off at the football game as soon as we finish here."

Still reluctant, I followed more slowly, gazing around in distaste at the mounted antlers, deer heads and pelts adorning the walls between racks of rifles and archery equipment. Except for the three of us, the store was empty.

"Have the other members of the Homecoming Court already been and gone?" I asked the man.

"Er…"

His hesitation reminded me to focus my emotion-sensing power on him. The second I did, I grabbed my aunt's arm.

"Let's go, Aunt Theresa," I said urgently. "This isn't—"

Moving with surprising quickness for a man his size, he stepped between us and the outer door. "No. I'm afraid I can't let you leave just yet…alien."

Aunt Theresa flinched. I tightened my grip on her arm before she could blurt out anything incriminating.

"What do you mean we can't leave?" I demanded, careful to sound both outraged and confused. "And *what* did you just call me?"

"You heard me. Alien." He turned the lock on the door, never taking his eyes off us. "Maybe you can hide it from everyone else, but not me. I shoulda guessed way back last year there was something *inhuman* about you—and especially Stuart, that boyfriend of yours."

I kept my confused look in place, fighting back the growing panic that threatened to cloud my thinking. "I have no idea what you're talking about, Mr…"

"Farmer. Ted Farmer"

That must be why he looked familiar. "Bryce's father?"

"That's right. The one your *alien* boyfriend cheated out of a college scholarship, stealing his quarterback spot last season. I shoulda believed Bryce when he said there was something odd about the Stuart kid. No *human* sophomore could've played like that. Plus he told me how Stuart knocked him out after a practice last fall…without leaving a mark on him. What did he use, some alien weapon?"

I snorted with all the derision I could muster. "Look, I'm sure Bryce was embarrassed about Rigel knocking him down, what with Bryce being both bigger *and* older than him. Did Bryce happen to tell you he was bullying *me* at the time? Rigel blocked him from grabbing me and he slipped on the bleachers, that's all. There was nothing *alien* about it, just Bryce being a jerk and Rigel catching him off-guard."

As I spoke, I moved slowly to one side, pulling Aunt Theresa along with me. I should be a lot faster and maybe even stronger than Mr. Farmer. If we could just get a little closer to the door…

"You can just stop right there, Miss Truitt—or whatever your real name is. I'd rather not have to use this." Reaching behind him as he spoke, he suddenly produced a wicked-looking handgun that must have been stuck in his back waistband.

"Maybe *you've* got some alien power to stop bullets but I don't expect your aunt does." He pointed the gun at her. "Unless you're one, too, Miz Truitt?"

Aunt Theresa gasped, her terror palpable. "Ted, think about what you're doing, what you're saying. You know perfectly well I've lived in Jewel all my life. I was born here. So were my parents." Though I could feel her trembling, she spoke calmly, reasonably.

Eyes narrowing, he huffed out a breath. "But this niece of yours, she's adopted, right? Nobody knows who her real parents are, that's what Bryce told me."

"What, and that makes me an alien?" I tried hard to sound more outraged than scared. "Lots of kids are adopted. Do you think we're *all* aliens? That's just crazy!"

"*Don't* call me crazy," he snapped, his face reddening. "Now, move away from the door, both of you. Go on. That's right, all the way to the back of the store."

Keeping hold of Aunt Theresa's arm, I backed up, not taking my eyes off him—or the gun that was still pointed at my aunt. The burst of frustrated, self-righteous fury I sensed from Mr. Farmer implied he'd been called crazy before—maybe lots of times. I didn't dare provoke him any further since he was clearly capable of violence. No wonder Bryce had been such a bully. He must have learned it at home.

"I, um, do need to get to the football game, Mr. Farmer." I tried to speak as reasonably, as calmly, as Aunt Theresa had a moment ago. "My friends will notice if I don't show up. They knew I was coming here first, so this will be the first place they'll look."

That wasn't true, unfortunately. I hadn't told Deb *why* my aunt was driving me because I didn't want her or Bri to think I was bragging.

"They won't find you—or hear you yell—even if they do

come out here. In there, both of you." He gestured with the gun toward an enormous steel door behind the back counter.

"Wait, you're planning to lock us in the freezer?" I let some of my fear show in my voice now, since any normal person *would* be scared. "Why not just shoot us, if you're going to kill us anyway?"

"Marsha!" Aunt Theresa hissed warningly.

Mr. Farmer laughed—a really unpleasant laugh. "It's a cooler, not a freezer. And I don't plan to kill you. Not before I get my proof, anyways. Once I have that, nobody will care what I do to you. Hell, they'll probably help."

"Proof? What proof?" I was genuinely mystified now.

"Tonight's game. I heard your uncle talking to his buddies at Green's last night. He said you and Stuart are both aliens and have some kind of weird alien link that gives...superpowers or something. Makes him stronger and faster, anyway.

"I called Bryce when I got home and sure enough, he said Stuart's worst games last year were when *you* weren't there— when you two were broke up. Bryce's friends at Jewel High say it's the same this year—Stuart's playing got a whole lot better after you two got back together. So I decided to conduct a little experiment."

Aunt Theresa and I exchanged glances. She was close to panic, making me wish I had Dr. Stuart's power to calm people with my touch. I was afraid any second she might blurt out something he'd *really* consider proof. So far, it sounded like all he had to go on was what he'd overheard from Uncle Louie. I needed to keep it that way.

"What kind of experiment?" If I kept talking, kept Mr. Farmer talking, maybe my aunt would just listen and not say anything. Besides, the more I knew, the better my chances were of figuring a way out of this.

"You stay here till the game is over. Bryce will let me know if your boy Stuart has an off game. If he does, I got some buddies who'll help me get the whole truth outta you. Then we'll have enough to take to the sheriff, the papers, everybody."

He reached past me to open the meat locker, keeping the gun trained on Aunt Theresa—which kept me from trying anything. My reflexes might be superhuman, but all he had to do was pull that trigger. Unfortunately, I couldn't *really* stop bullets.

"Now give me your purses, cell phones and whatever you have in your pockets—'specially you, missie. Can't have you calling anybody or using some alien teleportation device to escape."

Since he had a gun, we didn't argue, though I really hated giving up my omni. Not only could I have used it to contact someone on the Council to come get us, it would have kept us warm in the meat locker. He took it gingerly, then turned it over in his hand, examining it.

"Truitt's friends didn't believe him last night when he claimed this was from Mars—just laughed at him. Lucky for them he didn't know how to make it zap them, or whatever it does." He looked questioningly at me.

I shrugged, trying to look amused. "I never heard of anybody getting zapped by a flash drive. That's all it is. I bought it in Kokomo a couple months ago—I still have the receipt. If you let us go, I can show it to you tomorrow."

Scowling, he set it on the counter next to our purses, then reached past us to open the steel door. The blast of cold air made my aunt and me both shiver. Desperately, I tried one last time to talk him out of forcing us in there.

"You can't seriously think anyone will consider a football player having a bad game as evidence of something as bizarre as aliens? That's just—" I bit back the word "crazy" before it could slip out again.

Even so, his eyes blazed. "I ain't the only one been worried 'bout an alien invasion, not by a long shot. Everybody knows the government's been covering alien stuff up since the fifties, probably longer—Area 51 and those FEMA camps and whatnot. We just never had a chance to prove it. You're going to be my proof, Miss Martian Queen. Inside. Now."

He stepped back from the open cooler door and motioned again with the gun.

"Ted, please," Aunt Theresa pleaded. "You can't possibly—"

"Don't tell me what I can't do!" he shouted, practically shoving the gun in her face. "I know what everybody—including you—says about me in town, that I'm nothing but a drunk and a redneck. I can't wait till the fine people of Jewel find out oh-so-upstanding Theresa Truitt's been harboring an *alien* all these years."

I gently tugged on her arm. "Come on, Aunt Theresa. Maybe he'll let us go when he doesn't get that proof he's hoping for." At least he wouldn't be able to shoot us once we were behind the heavy steel door—and I'd have a chance to reach out to Rigel.

"That's right," he sneered. "Be a good little Martian and maybe they won't do anything worse than experiments on you." His laugh now held a distinctly maniacal edge. "See you after the game."

He slammed the door shut, plunging us into darkness. A click told me he'd locked it from the outside.

"Oh, Marsha, I'm so sorry I insisted we—" Aunt Theresa began, almost whimpering, but I hushed her.

"Let me listen for a minute, okay?" I heard heavy footfalls retreating, then a cell phone being dialed.

"Hey, Bryce? You at the high school yet? Okay, let me know when you get there. Once the game starts, you can call or text me updates on how it's going. Yeah, I got her right here. She won't be able to give Stuart any extra alien powers or whatever tonight.

Right. Oh, hey, keep an eye on her friends, too, and let me know if they leave the game early, okay? Yeah."

There was a beep as he hung up, then the footsteps came closer again. "Hey, you ladies just *chill* for the next two-three hours, okay?" he called through the door. "Maybe take a nap." With another insane-sounding laugh he stomped away again and the outer door opened and closed.

We were trapped.

10

Fusion

WHEN I TURNED BACK to my aunt, her fear hit me almost like a physical blow, it was so intense.

"Don't worry, Aunt Theresa, it'll be okay. You'll see. We just have to wait him out. He's bound to realize he doesn't have enough evidence to convince anybody of anything. If all he knows is whatever Uncle Louie said last night, we should be fine. None of his friends believed him, right?"

I heard her take a shaky breath in the darkness. "But...what about that proof he thinks he'll get tonight? If it's true that—?"

"I'm sure Rigel will play just fine. We do enhance each other, like I told you, but we were together a lot today, right up till the end of school. It's only when we have to stay apart—not touching —for days at a time that we start getting sick and weak. Like last Thanksgiving."

Okay, when we were separated on Mars it had happened faster than that, but the serum we'd been given then *might* still be working. Just to be safe, I'd better tell Rigel to play his absolute best tonight—if I could do it without worrying him so much he'd insist on coming to rescue me right away instead of playing at all.

"There must be a light switch or cord in here somewhere. Let's see if we can find it," I suggested, to distract my aunt from being so scared—and to keep her busy while I worked out how to word my thought-message to Rigel.

After about five minutes, she exclaimed, "I found a chain!" A second later, the welcome light of a single bare bulb filled the chilly meat locker.

Or maybe not so welcome. "Ew." I grimaced at the sight of two deer carcasses hanging near the back of the cooler and big trays of raw meat and sausages on shelves lining the walls. Maybe dark was better.

Aunt Theresa frowned at the carcasses, too. "Those had better be farmed," she commented. "Deer season doesn't start for weeks."

I snorted a half-laugh. "Do you really think Mr. Farmer cares? Hunting deer out of season is pretty minor stuff compared to kidnapping." I immediately regretted my words, because her fear spiked again.

"I...suppose you're right. Do you think he intends to...to kill us? Especially if he doesn't get his so-called proof, he won't want us going to the police..."

"No, Aunt Theresa, he won't. I promise."

I instilled every ounce of confidence possible into my tone, along with a bit of "push."

"I'd rather not do anything a, um, regular person can't do, since I don't want to give him *real* proof. But if that's what it takes to save our lives, I think I can take him."

She regarded me doubtfully. "How? He took your...what did you call it?"

"Omni. It's not a weapon anyway, though I could have used it to call for help. And keep us warm. But I'm a lot stronger and faster than I used to be, because of my bond with Rigel. Plus I know taekwondo."

"Shh!" She glanced at the big door.

"He's not close enough to hear. I heard him go outside a few minutes ago, after he called Bryce. I'll hear if he comes back."

Her eyebrows shot up. "Is that something else you can do that normal…I mean—"

"Yeah. We all tend to have extra-sensitive hearing, but nowadays mine—and Rigel's—is even better. Just like I haven't needed glasses since last fall. We *will* get out of this, Aunt Theresa. Please don't worry."

She nodded. Then shivered. I wished more than ever I still had my omni—or even a sweater.

"What time is it?" I asked after two or three more uncomfortable minutes passed.

She checked her watch. "A quarter to seven. The game will be beginning soon, won't it?"

"Yeah, kickoff's usually at seven. Why don't we grab some of those styrofoam meat trays—they don't look like they've been used—and sit on them? That'll be warmer than sitting on the cement, and three hours is a long time to stand."

I grabbed a big stack of trays off a shelf and spread them on the floor several deep. Gingerly, Aunt Theresa sat down and I did the same.

"That was very clever, Marsha. Thank you." She sounded surprised, like she always did when she complimented me.

I grinned, determined to keep her spirits up. "A leader has to be able to improvise—and plan. Give me a few minutes to think through all our options and I'll bet I can come up with some way to get us out of here."

"Oh. Of…of course." She looked positively impressed now.

Taking a deep breath, I shut my eyes and concentrated, focusing south and west, toward Jewel High—and Rigel.

Rigel? Can you hear me?

I waited. And waited. After a minute or two, I tried again. *Rigel?*

And again.

Rigel? Are you there?

M? It was faint but unmistakable. *We just finished warmup drills. Aren't you here yet? You sound kind of far away.*

I kind of am. It looks like I'm not going to be able to make it there for kickoff. But even if I don't get there at all, you need to play really, really well, okay?

As I feared, his next thought was laced with alarm. *Why? What's going on? Do I need to—*

No! I'm totally fine. I'll explain everything once the game's over, I promise. For now, just play the absolute best you can. Please, Rigel!

There was a long pause. Then, *Can't you tell me* now *what's going on? How can I concentrate on the game if I'm worrying about you?*

I sighed. I'd been afraid of this. *Okay. Remember how I wasn't sure if Uncle Louie would be able to keep his mouth shut? Well, he didn't. And now some crazy conspiracy theorist thinks if you have a bad game while I'm not there, it'll prove we're both aliens.*

You mean he's keeping you somewhere against your will? Keeping you from coming to the game?

Yes, but we're perfectly safe, I promise! As long as we make sure he doesn't get his so-called proof, I'm sure he'll let us go after the game.

Who's "we"? And where are you?

I hesitated. If I told him, I knew he'd be tempted to launch a rescue right away. And Mr. Farmer had told Bryce to keep an eye on all my friends…

Aunt Theresa is with me, though that wasn't part of his plan. I'll tell you where we are as soon as the game is over. We should be totally safe till then. If I think we need somebody to come get us sooner, I'll let you know right away.

Promise? I could sense his desperation.

I knew how he felt, since I'd experienced the same thing on his behalf more than once over the past year. But keeping the secret of Martians on Earth was way more important than my personal safety, so I infused all the confidence I could into my next thought.

Yes. I promise. We really are fine, Rigel. He just wants you to have a terrible game so he can point to that as evidence of his theory. If you don't play at all, he'll consider that even bigger proof and he'll use it to fire up all the other nut jobs paranoid about an alien takeover. We—you —have to make sure he can't do that.

Okay, he finally sent, with obvious reluctance. *I'll do all I can to make this my best game ever. For you. I love you, M. Please stay safe. For me.*

I will. I love you Rigel. I'll see you later tonight, I promise!

Once I was sure our connection was broken—Rigel probably had to get out on the field any second—I silently let out the breath I'd been holding and turned to Aunt Theresa, letting my relief show.

"I just remembered! I have something that will work as a fail-safe on the off-chance Mr. Farmer won't let us go after the game. When I got back to Earth, the *Echtran* Council insisted I have a microscopic tracker put in so if I was ever in danger someone could find me. I don't want to bring them here in force unless I have to, since that would just confirm Mr. Farmer's suspicion, but if worse comes to worst, I can activate it."

"And then what?"

"Then Mr. Cormac—my Bodyguard, remember?—will know exactly where I am. He'll contact a few others for backup and they'll come rescue us."

I willed her to believe me since I'd rather not tell her—or anyone—about Rigel's and my long-distance telepathy just yet.

Looking cautiously relieved, she nodded. "That…was very foresighted of them."

"Wasn't it?" Wondering if anything like I'd described actually existed, I summoned a bright smile. "Now all we have to do is try to stay warm…and wait."

The next two-plus hours shut in that creepy cooler with Aunt Theresa were among the strangest of my life—which was saying a lot.

She and I had lived together in the same house since I was four, but we'd hardly ever really *talked* with each other. Now there was nothing else to do. So, after several minutes of awkward silence…we talked.

Aunt Theresa spoke first. "Marsha, I never should have insisted we come here. You said from the first you thought the timing was odd for a photo shoot. I should have listened."

"No, this is way more my fault than yours. I should have trusted you when you said Uncle Louie wouldn't be able to resist talking about the whole Martian thing, but I told him anyway."

She managed a slight smile. "I'm afraid he's never been able to keep a secret, as long as I've known him. I did hope he'd show more discretion for something this important but he apparently just doesn't have it in him. Of course, it's possible he'd have begun suspecting sooner or later anyway."

"It definitely hasn't been easy keeping you guys from finding out this past year. Especially when you got mad at me for doing things that… Well, for things I couldn't explain."

For a long moment she looked at me, her brows furrowed. "Yes. Yes, I'm sure that must have been very difficult for you. Last year, when you sneaked out of the house at midnight to meet that boy—Rigel Stuart, I mean—at the arboretum—?"

"Okay, I'll admit that wasn't one of the smartest things I've done, but we were pretty desperate to talk to each other because of some Martian political stuff we'd just learned at his birthday party the night before."

I hadn't told her yet about Sean and the whole "destined Consort" thing, so I went on to explain how *fines* and pairings traditionally worked in Nuath and why it mattered so much to some *Echtrans*. "But like I've told the Council, with everyone relocating to Earth over the next few decades, there are lots of old traditions that will have to change. That Consort one, for sure."

Her eyes had gone wider and wider as I talked but now she shook her head. "I can see why you were so upset. At the time, I truly believed Sean O'Gara would be a better influence than the Stuart boy. Lili—"

"Yes, I'm sure Mrs. O'Gara did all she could to convince you of that—and she can be super convincing. It's…kind of a power of hers." I didn't mention I now had that power, too. Best to keep a *few* secrets.

Aunt Theresa blinked. "Really? Hm. Now I feel I've been quite gullible." She hmphed, sounding more like herself than she had since we'd been shut into the cooler. "No wonder she encouraged me to keep such a close eye on you after that incident."

"What, like you weren't strict enough already?"

I felt a little gullible myself now, remembering how outraged Mrs. O had acted about the way my aunt treated me while actually encouraging her to be stricter. Which prompted me to ask something I'd never dared before.

"Why *have* you always been so strict, Aunt Theresa? Even when I was little, way before I had to hide any Martian stuff from you, I felt like you never really trusted me."

She didn't answer right away. Focusing, I sensed a conflict raging inside her that had nothing to do with the danger we were in right now. After a moment, she gave a little nod.

"I suppose I may as well tell you, though for years I've tried to convince myself… I can't recall if I ever mentioned that I had a sister?"

It was my turn to blink. "No. I'm sure I'd remember something like that. Why—?"

"She died quite young, at the age of fourteen. I was just seventeen at the time myself."

Though her voice was nearly emotionless, her feelings were anything but. I sensed grief, resentment, anger…and guilt.

"What happened?" I prompted quietly.

Aunt Theresa heaved a sigh. "As the youngest, Janet was always the apple of our mother's eye. Both our parents, really. As far as they were concerned, she could do no wrong. She was their perfect little angel, while I…I was expected to be the responsible one. To keep a protective eye on her whenever we were at school or otherwise away from our parents."

"That doesn't seem very fair. So they were way stricter with you than with her?"

A small, sad smile touched her lips. "That's putting it rather mildly. My slightest infraction was invariably punished, so I became very careful never to commit any. Janet, on the other hand, realized early on that she could get away with nearly anything. On the few occasions when I tried to warn our parents about her behavior for fear she might land herself in real trouble, they punished me rather than her. Said I was jealous. A tattletale."

She swallowed, her smile gone.

"I…I should have kept warning them anyway. They might have been able to prevent what happened, had I been able to convince them. But—" Sadly, she shook her head.

"What did happen?" I asked, though now I dreaded the answer.

"By the time she started high school, Janet had fallen in with a bad crowd, many of them older. She was always the popular one, you see, though she was three years younger than I. The pretty one. I used to warn her about the boys she spent time with, but she only ever laughed at me. Then one Saturday night she went joy riding with three older boys. There was a terrible car accident out on state road 311. She and one of the boys were killed and the other two boys hospitalized. The police said later they had all been drinking and drag racing…"

Her voice trailed off. The pain I felt from her was nearly as strong as if it had just happened last week.

"I'm…I'm so sorry, Aunt Theresa. But it sounds like you did all you could. If your parents had only listened—"

"My mother didn't see it that way. She blamed me for not keeping a closer eye on Janet, for not somehow preventing what happened. She…my parents… were never the same afterward. Mother went into a decline and died two years later. Father started drinking and eventually lost his business and our house."

I knew which house it was. She'd pointed it out to me more than once—a beautiful Victorian mansion at least four times the size of ours, a block past the courthouse. The historical society owned it now and it housed the Jewel Chamber of Commerce.

"I'm sorry," I repeated. "I never knew."

She shook her head, almost fiercely. "No. Of course not. Almost no one does. Father managed to hush up the truth about the drinking and the boys—he was still quite a prominent citizen back then. Most believe to this day that my sister was a completely innocent victim. The…the whole town mourned her."

I tried to imagine how Aunt Theresa must have felt back then, only a year older than I was now. It wasn't easy, but sensing her emotions helped.

"So that's why you were always so strict with me? So I… wouldn't end up like your sister?" It did sort of make sense now.

She nodded. "That's what I told myself. And Louie. After seeing what my sister's death did to my parents, I was secretly relieved when it turned out Louie and I were unable to have children. Not that I could admit that to anyone, even when they pitied me. *Choosing* to remain childless simply…wasn't done, you see. Not in Jewel, not back then."

"And then I was suddenly left on your hands."

No wonder she'd never acted like she wanted me around. She really hadn't. Though it hurt to have that confirmed after suspecting it all these years, I was glad to finally learn *why.* It helped a little.

"Yes. At first—for quite a while, actually—I considered your being orphaned a cruel trick of fate. My punishment for being happy *not* to have children of my own. I realize now, with the distance of years, how terribly unfair that was to you, especially when you'd so recently lost your second set of parents. Any normal woman would have felt sorry for you, smothered you with attention, given you anything you wanted."

My aunt pressed her lips together for a moment before continuing.

"But whenever I was tempted to give in to sentiment, I would remember Janet. She had green eyes too, though not so green as yours. So when you would look up at me, pleading for some treat or even a hug, I'd think of how Janet used to wheedle our mother into giving her whatever she wanted—and how terribly that turned out."

She lapsed into silence. Thinking over all she'd just told me, I realized that in a twisted sort of way her strictness, even her coldness toward me, had been out of genuine concern.

"Thank you for telling me, Aunt Theresa. I…I get it now."

"Do you?" The plea in her faded gray eyes startled me. "I should have realized years ago that you were nothing like Janet, but by then old habits… And now, to learn you were so important all along, a princess! How you must resent the way I've treated you all these years."

I had, of course. Lots of times. But now I said, "You didn't know. How could you, when I didn't even know? Anyway, that's all in the past now, right?"

"Will you…can you forgive me, then? I've had to face things about myself these past few days that I…don't particularly like. I truly want to do better by you in the future, and not only because of…of who you really are."

"Of course I forgive you."

I wasn't sure who moved first, but suddenly we were hugging, really hugging, in a way I couldn't remember ever doing in all the years she'd been my aunt. It felt…

Well, okay, weird.

But also wonderful.

11

Refraction

IT WAS MAYBE AN HOUR LATER–THE game must have been well into the fourth quarter by then—when I heard Mr. Farmer shouting. Exchanging a quick glance with Aunt Theresa, I jumped up and hurried to the door to listen. Had Rigel somehow figured out where I was after all—?

"You gotta be kidding me, Bryce! That's impossible. I saw how that kid played last year. How can he be doing even *better* without his alien girlfriend there?"

Straining my Martian hearing for all it was worth, I could just make out Bryce's voice on the other end.

"I should've known everything you told me was nuts, no matter how much I wanted to believe it. You've still got her there, right? Well, Jewel's ahead by forty-seven points, so they're running a continuous clock. Stuart hasn't missed a single pass, hasn't been sacked once, and has more yards rushing than all the other players on *both* teams put together. Face it, Dad, this was just another one of your crackpot conspiracy fantasies."

"Don't you dare talk to me like that, boy!" Mr. Farmer thundered. "One of these days you'll see I was right all along—about everything! Now get yourself out here and help me deal with—"

"No way, Dad! I'm done. I want nothing to do with whatever you're planning—and if you end up in jail again over this, I'm not bailing you out this time."

"Bryce! Bryce!" But apparently his son had already hung up.

Mr. Farmer started swearing so loudly even Aunt Theresa could hear him. It sounded like he was getting angrier and angrier the longer he went on. And he was heading our way.

I quickly retreated to my aunt's side. "He's coming, and he's pissed."

"Then your…Rigel Stuart…wasn't able to play well without you there after all?"

"Just the opposite. Sounds like he had the game of his life and Mr. Farmer's not happy about it. Just a sec…"

Rigel! I sent urgently. *Are you there?*

M! You sound really scared. What's going on?

You'd better send help after all—right away! I think Mr. Farmer's about to lose it, and I don't know what he might be capable of. We're at the Bulls-Eye Whitetail Ranch, a couple miles northeast of the school, shut in the meat cooler. Is the game over yet?

Last few seconds counting down now…and there's the whistle.

Good! Tell your parents, the O'Garas, Cormac, everybody you can, to get here as soon as— Crap, he's coming in!

Aunt Theresa had scrambled to her feet, too, at the sound of Mr. Farmer unlocking the cooler door.

"I just activated my tracker," I whispered to her. "Help should be coming soon. Meanwhile, let's try to calm him down. Keep him talking, buy some time."

Before she could respond, the steel door swung open. When I saw Mr. Farmer's face, I knew I hadn't messaged Rigel a moment too soon. His eyes were wide and crazed, his face scarlet with the fury that radiated from him.

"How did you do it?" he yelled at me. "You must have something I missed, some long-distance alien gizmo or power you used from here. There's no other way—!"

"What happened, Mr. Farmer? I promise, we haven't done anything at all. How could we, from in here?" Pulling Aunt Theresa with me, I backed well out of arm's reach—though not out of reach of the gun he was holding.

"Stuart…Bryce said…even without you there…"

He was so upset he was having trouble getting the words out. I sensed almost equal parts unreasoning fury and frustration—not much I could work with. I tried anyway.

"I'm sorry you're disappointed, Mr. Farmer. I'm sure whatever you heard my uncle saying last night must have made it sound like—"

"Sound like, nothing! He flat-out said you're an alien. A Martian. Stuart too. No matter how you try to twist it, I heard what I heard. Now tell me how you did it!"

"Did what, Mr. Farmer? What is it you think I did? I'll…I'll try to undo it, whatever it is, if you think it might help."

He glared at me, taking a step forward. "You can't undo it, it's too late for that. Bryce told me Stuart played football like some NFL all-star tonight. I just want to know *how*?"

Swallowing, I shrugged, inching backward some more. "He's just…a really good football player. That was true even before he came to Jewel. I wish I could take credit, but I can't. Any more than I can take credit—or blame—for anything my Uncle Louie says when he's had a few beers. He's always liked to tell wild stories and…and play practical jokes on his friends. He was probably just messing with them last night."

I kept my voice as calm as I could, projecting every bit of "push" at him I could muster, willing him to believe me, to relax. I'd made it work on Sean and Rigel last year, when they'd both been spoiling for a fight…

Incredibly, it started to work now, too—at least a little. Mr. Farmer was still furious but uncertainty began to creep in, dulling the edge of his anger.

"You're saying it was a *joke*? Why? Because he knew I was listening? Knew I—?"

"I'm sure it had nothing to do with you, Mr. Farmer. He probably just wanted to laugh at his buddies if they bought into his story. He...he does stuff like that all the time. Really." If I could just keep him talking until Rigel and the others got here...

"She's right," Aunt Theresa unexpectedly chimed in, doing her best to sound as reasonable as I had, though I could tell she was still terrified. "My husband has always been prone to...to exaggeration, even fabrication. Particularly when he's been drinking. It...it pains me to admit it, but it would be just like him to make up a story like the one you apparently overheard last night."

"It's true, Mr. Farmer," I quickly agreed. "He, um, even tries to convince customers at the car lot that he used to be a race car driver. Or a, uh, movie star." Unfortunately, I wasn't as good at this sort of thing as Molly. My words sounded lame even to me.

Mr. Farmer was still glowering but I felt his anger recede slightly as uncertainty and embarrassment crept in. He didn't lower the gun, though.

"Can't say I know Louie Truitt all that well, but he shouldn't lie to people like that, especially about something this important. It ain't right."

"No. No, it's not," Aunt Theresa agreed emphatically. "By now, most of his friends know better than to take everything he says at face value. As you don't know him well, it's understandable how you might have been misled."

"You didn't hear him. He really sounded like he meant it."

"I'm sure he did. He can be very convincing."

There was a brief silence, then I tentatively said, "Now that you realize what happened, Mr. Farmer, will you please let my aunt take me home? We're sure to have been missed by now."

"What, so you can tell the police? Spread it all over town how I was hoodwinked?"

"No, we won't tell anybody," I assured him, using my "push" again. "Please, just let us go!"

For a moment he hesitated, then shook his head. "It's too risky. But if you told people you were coming here, I better take you someplace else before I— Come on, outside. Now."

He backed out of the cooler, gesturing with the gun for us to follow. We'd only taken a few steps into the blessedly warmer store when several car doors suddenly slammed outside. Immediately, Mr. Farmer wheeled to face the outer door, swinging the pistol around with him.

"Who's out there? Did you somehow call the cops anyway?"

"Of course not!" I exclaimed. "How could we?"

Then urgently, to Rigel, *Is that you? He just let us out of the meat locker but he's got a gun.* I glanced at the racks of rifles along the walls and another leaning against the door frame—probably loaded. *Lots of guns! Tell everybody to be really careful—and to not say anything incriminating.*

Got it, he sent back.

"Then who—?" Mr. Farmer glared suspiciously at my aunt and me, then back at the door. He apparently noticed the rifle then, too, because he took two quick steps toward it.

Just then the door slammed open and Rigel, still in his football jersey, burst through, Cormac right behind him. An instant later they were followed by Rigel's parents, Mr. and Mrs. O'Gara, Sean, Molly, and, amazingly, my Uncle Louie.

"Wait!" My command, strengthened by my Royal "push," was aimed at all of them, Mr. Farmer included. To my surprise, every single one of them froze in their tracks.

I ran forward to put a hand on Mr. Farmer's arm, though not

the one that held the gun, since I didn't want to startle him into pulling the trigger while it was pointing at Rigel. My touch must have given him a static shock, though, because he flinched, then swung around to stare at me, his eyes wide.

"So it's true after all! You almost had me convinced it wasn't, with your…your alien mind control, but—"

"Of course it's not true, Mr. Farmer," I said, desperation marring the calm I was trying to project. "These are my friends, who knew I was coming here. I'm sure they just got worried when I didn't show up at the game, like I said they would. Right, guys?"

The Stuarts and O'Garas nodded immediately. Rigel and Cormac still looked ready to tackle Mr. Farmer, but catching my eye, they finally nodded, too.

Amazingly, Uncle Louie was the first to speak. "Hey, Ted, what's with the gun? Don't tell me you believed all that stuff I was telling the guys last night at Green's, about aliens?"

He stepped forward, actually shouldering Rigel and Cormac aside to get between them and the pistol. My uncle's face was a little paler than usual, but he otherwise did a surprisingly good job of hiding the fear he broadcast to me.

"Look, I'm really sorry if you took that story the wrong way. Guess you didn't hear the setup, huh? It was just an idea for a TV show I was planning to send to a guy I met last month—a guy who stopped by the car lot—who works for a studio out in California. I had the details all worked out, though of course I'd have changed the names and all. I just used Marsha here as an example. My buddies thought it sounded stupid, though, so I probably won't bother writing it all up after all."

Keeping my hand on Mr. Farmer's arm, I forced enthusiasm into my voice. "I think you still should, Uncle Louie! Who knows? Maybe it'll be a hit."

Again, uncertainty warred with Mr. Farmer's fear and anger —but then he violently shook his head.

"I don't buy it." Gripping his gun more tightly, he glared around at all of us, eyes narrowed. "No. I think you're *all* aliens, every one of you, here to shut me up. But I won't shut up! Not unless you kill me. And you won't do that without me taking at least one of you with me—starting with your queen, here. The world needs to know the truth!"

He tried to pull out of my grasp, to turn the gun on me, but he'd barely moved when Rigel darted forward with incredible speed to put his hand on top of mine still gripping Mr. Farmer's left arm. The resulting electrical jolt caused Mr. Farmer's eyes to go super wide for an instant, then he slumped to the floor, unconscious.

Now Rigel wrapped a protective arm around my shoulders, relief flooding us both—to be immediately followed by a whole different worry.

"We didn't...didn't..." I began.

Swiftly, Dr. Stuart knelt by Mr. Farmer's sprawled form to check the pulse at his throat. "No. He's merely stunned. That was...very quick thinking, Rigel."

"It was indeed," Cormac agreed, removing the gun from Mr. Farmer's hand. "Excellency, are you unharmed?"

I nodded. "Aunt Theresa and I nearly had him convinced it was all just a wild story of Uncle Louie's, but he still wasn't willing to let us go. In fact...I think he might have been about to silence us both for good. He's pretty obviously nuts."

"Indeed," said Mr. O'Gara. "But he clearly learned at least part of the truth. From you, I presume?" He regarded Uncle Louie with a raised brow.

Shamefaced now, Uncle Louie nodded. "Yeah. This whole thing is my fault. Marsha told me a dozen times how important it was to keep everything secret, but it all just seemed so...cool, you know? I figured with the way these new folks are already starting to prop up Jewel's economy, people wouldn't mind if they happened to be, um, aliens. I never thought anyone would—" He broke off at everyone's stares, dropping his eyes.

"I, um, get it now," he mumbled. "Telling my buddies was really, really dumb—even though *they* didn't believe me. You two could have…could have been killed." He sent an apologetic, pleading look at Aunt Theresa.

"You never do think ahead, Louie," she snapped, clearly not in a forgiving mood just yet. "How many times have I told you—"

I interrupted before she could launch into full lecture mode. "We can talk about this when we get home, okay? Right now, we need to decide what to do about Mr. Farmer before he wakes up. Can we…make him forget all this?"

Dr. Stuart stood from where she'd still been kneeling next to him. "I'm not a trained Mind Healer, nor do I have the equipment necessary for memory erasure. However, I do have something in my bag that will make his recollections of the past day or two extremely fuzzy. Even if he eventually manages to piece together his recent experiences, I can't imagine he'll convince anyone else to believe him."

"That should work," I said. "Even Bryce thinks his dad is a crackpot. I heard him say so on the phone."

"Yes, it's been common knowledge for a long time that Ted Farmer has…issues," Aunt Theresa agreed. "Not that that in any way excuses what my husband did."

The look she shot Uncle Louie made him redden. There was going to be one heck of a reckoning when they got home, no doubt about it.

Rigel still had his arm around me. "You positive you're okay?" he murmured when his mom went back out to the car for her medical bag.

"I'm fine. Still a little cold, but I'm warming up now." I smiled up at him. Then another thought occurred to me.

How did you explain to everyone that you knew where to find us? Did you have to tell them about our—?

No. I was about to, then had the idea to say you left a message on my cell that I didn't see until after the game ended. Pretty sure they bought it.

Good. I hope there's never a reason we'll be glad we kept that secret, but…you never know.

Just then, Mr. Farmer started to groan, which had the effect of mobilizing everyone else. Cormac collected the rifle by the door and took it outside, along with the pistol. I found the cabinet where Mr. Farmer had stashed Aunt Theresa's purse and my omni. By the time Dr. Stuart returned a moment later with her black bag, the store looked like no one else had ever been there.

Leaning down, Rigel's mom smeared some kind of salve on Mr. Farmer's upper lip. He immediately stopped groaning and relaxed again, breathing deeply.

"That should keep him out for another twenty or thirty minutes," she said. "He'll be very confused when he wakes, but otherwise fine. With any luck, he'll think he passed out from drinking too much. I noticed a great number of beer bottles in the trash can just outside."

To strengthen that impression, Rigel went out and grabbed a few, putting several empty bottles on the back counter and another on the floor next to Mr. Farmer.

Then, after one last glance around, we all headed outside. We should be well away before he woke up.

12

Brilliance

AUNT THERESA INSISTED Uncle Louie ride with her—probably so she could start lecturing him right away. He didn't protest, so Mr. O drove Uncle Louie's car back while Mrs. O took Sean and Molly home in theirs. When the Stuarts offered me a ride, I quickly accepted. Not only did Rigel and I feel a desperate need to be together after our scare, I had no desire to hear the tongue-lashing my uncle was about to get.

Climbing into the back seat of the Stuarts' SUV, I leaned contentedly against Rigel. I didn't care that he still reeked of sweat from the game. He was my knight in shining armor—though his pads, helmet and cleats were all piled on the floor of the car.

"So, it sounds like you managed a pretty good game after all," I commented to him as we headed down the long gravel drive back to the state road.

He gave me that crooked grin I loved so much. *After what you told me, I figured it was the best way to keep you safe.* Then, out loud, "Yeah, though of course I thought you were in the stands—at least until halftime. Wish I'd thought to check my phone then. We could have rescued you sooner."

"Just as well," I said. "Bryce was there, keeping an eye on all my friends as well as the game so he could report back to his dad. If you'd all left at the half, Mr. Farmer would have known right away something was up, and who knows what he might have done. It must have been awkward, though, all of you rushing off the second the game ended?"

Usually, it took Rigel a while to extricate himself from all the Jewel fans eager to congratulate him after a good game—and from what I'd heard Bryce tell his father, this had been his best ever.

"The cause absolutely justified it," Dr. Stuart said, "though I'll admit we had other reasons for wishing to make a quick exit."

The irritation that accompanied her words—echoed by her husband—immediately concerned me. "What happened? Was another one of the new arrivals rude to you guys at the game?"

"Not rude, precisely," Mr. Stuart replied with obvious reluctance. "It was more that they behaved as though we weren't there at all, even when we attempted to speak to them."

Dr. Stuart nodded. "It was rather, ah, uncomfortable, to say the least. Though, as I said last night, I'm sure in time they'll come around."

I started getting pissed all over again. "Let me check something." I pulled out my omni. If Kyna *still* hadn't answered me…

She had. I played the waiting message aloud.

"I must say, I'm impressed, Excellency." Kyna's voice was loud enough for everyone in the car to hear. "As the Royals on the Council were the ones to suggest you compose any followup statement, I see no reason to consult them before authorizing this to go out over MARSTAR. I'll see that it's sent within the hour."

"What statement is that?" Mr. Stuart asked, clearly startled. "I wasn't told that anything would be broadcast via MARSTAR tonight."

"Just a little addendum to the one the Council sent out last week. Let me check if it's actually gone out yet." I tapped the setting on my omni to display MARSTAR messages. "Ah, it looks like Kyna sent it about half an hour ago."

Dr. Stuart glanced curiously over her shoulder at me. "This is a statement you composed yourself, Excellency?"

"Yes. That's what the Royals on the Council suggested when I insisted they correct the glaring omission in their last one. I'll double check what was actually sent—like I *should* have done last week. Do you want me to read it to you?"

"Please do," Mr. Stuart said.

I pulled up the text of the most recent MARSTAR transmission and started reading aloud.

"The following is a statement from the *Echtran* Council. Last Saturday, in our haste to assure everyone that we no longer had anything to fear from the Grentl, we neglected to mention the vital role Rigel Stuart played in averting that danger. As a critical element of the defense our Scientists devised, Rigel Stuart and Sovereign Emileia both agreed to risk their own safety, perhaps even their lives, in order to use a recently discovered aspect of their *graell* bond to prevent what would surely have been a cataclysmic loss of power and life on Earth. We apologize for the delay in recognizing Rigel Stuart's essential contribution and wish to extend our extreme gratitude to both him and our Sovereign for their selfless bravery on everyone's behalf."

Mr. Stuart drove in silence for a minute or two, then said, "But...didn't you say *you* wrote the statement, Excellency?"

"I did. But if you remember, the Council never said anything about how I should word it. They've written and sent out plenty of statements in *my* name over the past year, so I figured it would be okay to send out this one in theirs."

"A rather clever approach, I must say." Dr. Stuart sounded both surprised and impressed. "I can't help hoping it will help—" Her cell phone chimed and she broke off.

"Yes? You have? Why, thank you, Gwendolyn, that's very big of you. Yes, I'll tell him."

She turned back around, now wearing a broad smile. "That was Gwendolyn Gannett. It seems the *Echtran Enquirer* has been getting some rather, ah, unpleasant feedback over the past several minutes. She asked me to convey her apology to Rigel for publishing that article last week without sufficiently checking her facts first."

Rigel and I grinned at each other.

"Bet you and Dad get a few apologies, too," he predicted, then checked his own cell phone. "Huh, looks like I've already received a couple of 'I'm sorry' emails myself, judging from the subject lines."

By the time we reached my house, emails and more calls had begun pouring in, all to say how sorry people were for misjudging Rigel and his parents. The growing relief I sensed from Dr. and Mr. Stuart was palpable. Clearly they'd each received a *lot* more insults and veiled threats than either had been willing to let on to the other.

"You did it," Rigel told me as he walked me to my door. "I can't imagine why I ever doubted you. I'm starting to wonder if there's any problem you can't solve."

I laughed. "You helped a lot, just like you do with everything —not to mention you probably saved my life tonight. Again. Even if Mr. Farmer wasn't planning to kill us, I'd be a pretty sucky Sovereign without you."

He shook his head. "Nah, you'd be great. But if you think working together on everything from now on will make you an even better one, I won't argue." Leaning in, he kissed me and, like always, I melted.

"You know," he murmured after a long, blissful moment, "with all these changes in Jewel, we're probably facing some pretty interesting times over the next few months—or years."

I grinned up at him. "Probably so. But as long as we're facing them together, we don't have a thing to worry about."

Keep reading for a preview of *The Girl From Mars*, book 5 in the **Starstruck** series!

The Girl From Mars (preview)

1

caidpel (KAYD-pel): *predominant sport played in Nuath, combining elements of the Irish sports of hurling and Gaelic football*

"Kira! I'm open!" My teammate Brady's call comes from across the *caidpel* field as two opposing players box me in.

Whirling to face him, I toss the ball from my hand to my *camman*, then use the stick to flick it his way over my opponents' heads. Brady barely has to stretch to catch the *schlitur* on a dead run toward the other team's goal. My way no longer blocked, I'm free to assist. As I streak down the *caidpel* pitch, the opposing goalposts loom up like a giant letter "A" with two crossbars, one above the other.

Brady lobs the ball toward the middle goal, between the two crossbars, five feet above the goalie's head. Not high enough. She extends her stick and jumps, deflecting it at the last second, but now I'm in position.

I leap in front of the man she's aiming for, knocking his *camman* aside with my left hand as I snag the ball in my right. Two quick steps, then I hurl the ball twice as high as Brady did. The *schlitur* sails through the small, triangular goal at the top, between the short upper crossbar and the pointed peak where the two posts converge twenty feet above the ground.

Five points! Seconds later the final chime sounds, ending the game with our team up 12-10 over the Healers.

My teammates converge on me, cheering wildly. "You did it, Kira!" screams Leitis, our goalie and my best friend on the team.

"Again," adds Brady, grinning at me over the top of Leitis's head. "Was a good day for the Ags when you joined us, Kira. Glad now I didn't make that three-pointer and throw us into overtime. Gave you a chance to go for the win. Well done!"

"Thanks." I grin back at him.

This is only my second season in the elite Senior *Caidpel* League, though I started playing on Hollydoon's girls' team when I turned twelve, nearly five years ago. Playing *caidpel*, even becoming one of Nuath's top players, might not be as world-changing as helping the Resistance was, but I still love it. Especially at moments like this, when I've just helped advance the Agricultural *fine*'s team into the playoffs.

Our green-clad fans start streaming onto the pitch to congratulate the players—especially me. Though I enjoy the adulation, seeing so many of my teammates being hugged by their families is a sharp reminder that my own didn't come. Never come.

Dad claims it's because the crowds spook Mum so much. Maybe it's true. She's never really been herself since Faxon's goons arrested her last year, two weeks before the dictator was overthrown. I should probably cut her more slack.

Retrieving my smile, I turn to a few younger fans thrusting their tablets toward me. I'm autographing the last one when I spot my little sister making her way toward me through the crowd. Scanning the area behind her, I see no sign of our parents.

"Hey, Adina. Did you come by yourself?"

"I came with Bronwyn's family. They figured I wouldn't want to miss your big game and they were right—you were awesome!"

I return her hug, absurdly touched. "Thanks, Sprout. You want to stick around and celebrate with the team? Coach said something about Sheelah's."

Adina's amber eyes widen at the name of the best restaurant in Newlyn—one of the best in Nuath, in fact. "Oh, wow, Sheelah's! But…I better not. The water dispenser in the sheep pen has been glitching lately and Mum never remembers to check it. Besides, I said I'd be home for dinner."

"You and your sheep." I ruffle my sister's short blonde hair.

While my parents and I have the skills with plants typical of most Ags, Adina has always had a special affinity for animals. Dad sometimes teases that Adina is a throwback to the time before Horticulture and Husbandry split into separate Agricultural sub-*fines*, five or six hundred years ago.

"I'll see you later then, okay?" I say. "Tell Mum and Dad not to wait dinner. And thank Bronwyn's folks for bringing you."

When the happy crowd finally disperses a little while later, our team heads to Sheelah's for our celebratory dinner. Coach assures us he called ahead to reserve their party room, but when we arrive the owner tells him it's already taken.

"But…I just called to confirm fifteen minutes ago," Coach protests. "You said you were holding that room for us."

The man, both shorter and noticeably pudgier than the average Nuathan, shrugs apologetically. "Sorry about that. They arrived just ahead of you, so what could I do?"

He jerks a thumb over his shoulder toward the archway leading into the room in question—the only one large enough to accommodate our whole team. Looking, I spot the unmistakeable tall, copper-headed figure of Sean O'Gara, the Sovereign's future Consort, laughing and talking with a dozen other guys around the same age. They all look pleased with themselves for pulling rank to snag the best room—the room that was *supposed* to be ours.

Even as I watch, Sean O'Gara turns his head and spots our team, still hovering by the door. Nudging a couple of his buddies, he grins widely and gives us a cocky thumbs-up. Gloating. Arrogant, Royal *twilly*.

"Seriously?" I say to our coach. "They bumped us for the Sovereign's lapdog and his Royal friends? They don't even need a room that big!"

"Shh!" Coach hisses at me. "Do you want to get us all in trouble?" Then, more loudly, "C'mon, everybody, we'll celebrate with fish and chips next door instead. My treat."

There's quite a bit of grumbling as we file back out, but no one dares protest too loudly. I glance back over my shoulder as I leave the restaurant and see Consort Sean still grinning at us, like he's daring us to try to oust him and his gang of Royals from the room *we* reserved.

"Jerks," I mutter. "They're as bad as Faxon's favorites used to be, lording it over everyone else."

The only one close enough to overhear is Brady, who immediately falls into step beside me. "You still miss it, don't you?" He slants a glance down at me with those dark blue eyes that make all the girls swoon.

I look up at him, startled. "Miss—? You mean…when we were still working to change things and *caidpel* was more than just a game?"

Brady is the only other member of our team who used the sport as cover to help the Resistance last year, when Faxon was still making everyone miserable. Our matches and practices take us all over Nuath, so it was easy to pass messages without Faxon's *bullochts*—who were everywhere—getting suspicious.

He nods. "I'm not criticizing, you're playing better than ever this season. But I can tell you don't have quite the same fire you did then. Am I wrong?"

For a second I don't answer, then I shake my head. "Not wrong. But we're supposed to be happy about it, right? The Resistance did what it set out to do—got rid of Faxon. Brought back the Sovereign." I can't quite keep the bitterness out of my voice on that last word.

Brady keeps watching me, not saying anything else until the team is busy placing their orders at the fish and chips counter. Then, softly, "What if I told you there are still ways to make a difference?"

"What do you mean?" I whisper back. "How?"

"Ask me tomorrow, after our practice in Monaru. 'K?"

I nod eagerly and he moves off. Leitis immediately takes his place at my side.

"Ooh, that looked a bit intense, Kira. You and Brady, eh?"

"Nah, just talking game strategy." I can't claim I'm not attracted to him. But so is every other girl on the team, along with half the female population of Nuath, drooling over him on the feeds.

Leitis sighs, looking over her shoulder after Brady. "He can talk strategy to *me* any time he wants, whether it's to do with *caidpel* or not," she says with a wink.

If I'm honest with myself, I feel the same way. But handsome as Brady is, at the moment I'm more interested in hearing whatever he's going to tell me tomorrow than in starting a romance.

"C'mon," I say to Leitis. "We'd better get our orders in before they run out of fresh chips."

Riding the zipper home to Hollydoon an hour later, I puzzle over Brady's cryptic words: *make a difference*. How?

Sure, there are things I'd change if I could. Because, no matter what my mother says, Nuath is nothing like I thought it would be once Faxon was gone.

Okay, maybe things aren't as bad as when people got hauled from their homes in the dead of night never to be seen again. And Faxon's *bullochts* are no longer roaming around taking whatever —or whoever—they want while supposedly "protecting" our villages. But while everything might have improved for those in the upper *fines*, not a whole lot has changed for the rest of us, other than feeling a little safer.

For instance, there's still no direct zipper from Newlyn to Hollydoon, which means I have to change in Thiaraway. Slinging my school bag over my shoulder, I get off my *tapacarr* and head across the main terminal to catch the next one home. As I swing by the big screen to check departure times, slightly raised voices off to my left catch my attention.

"How do we know you don't have anything good in there if you don't let us look?" I hear a male voice saying in a hectoring tone.

"Yeah," says another. "Open it up. Let's see what you've got."

Frowning, I glance over and see two guys about my age picking on someone much smaller than they are—with short, blond hair.

"Adina?" Outraged and furious, I barrel toward the group but realize halfway there that the blond kid is a boy, not my sister. Even so, I don't slacken my pace.

"What's the problem here?" I yell in the same voice I use to shout out plays on the *caidpel* pitch.

The two bigger boys whip around to glare at me. "None of your business, Ag," the taller one sneers, eyeing the green uniform I'm still wearing. "Just move along."

"I don't think so." I keep moving forward. "Not until you tell me why you're hassling this kid."

"He's got something we want," says the stockier boy. "Don't you, kid?"

"No!" The younger boy sounds scared. "I told you, all I have in here is my school stuff. Those omnis you saw earlier weren't mine, they were ones my dad repaired for their owners. I already delivered them."

"Then you won't mind if we take a look." The tall boy reaches for the kid's pack.

I push right up between them. "Let me guess, your dads used to work for Faxon and you think it's still okay to bully people? It's not. Knock it off unless you want everyone to know your families are still sympathizers."

There were penalties in place for that now, though I wasn't sure how strictly they were enforced.

"Shows what you know." The shorter, heavier set boy smirks at me. "My dad happens to be the Acting Under-Minister of Culture, not some filthy Faxon holdover."

"That's right," the skinny dark-haired one affirms. "So an Ag like you can't touch us. Playing on some stupid sports team doesn't make you *that* special."

Royals. I should have guessed. If anything, my opinion of them sinks lower.

"How do you think your parents will feel if word gets out their sons are shaking kids down right here in Thiaraway? That'll play great on the feeds. They love scandals like that."

I'm totally ready to get physical if that threat doesn't work… but it does.

"C'mon, Zach." The stocky one puts an urgent hand on his friend's shoulder.

The taller one glares at me for a second, then shrugs. "Yeah.

This kid's not worth our time anyway. You both better watch your step, though. We'll be watching."

"So will the media," I call after them as they hurry off. Then I turn to the blond boy. "You okay?"

He nods. "Thanks. Those two are the biggest bullies in school. Dunno what they'd have done if you—" Breaking off, he stares at me, apparently taking in my uniform, my face, for the first time. "Whoa! You're…are you Kira Morain?"

"Um, yeah. Why?"

"I caught the last half of tonight's game on the feeds," he says excitedly, his eyes shining now. "That last goal was brilliant! My family's Maintenance *fine*, Mechanics. No *caidpel* team, so we've always supported the Ags. Wait till I tell them I met you in person! Boy, will my brother be jealous."

I have to stifle a laugh. At least he seems to be over his fright. "You want me to autograph something so you can prove it?" I ask, half teasing.

"Oh, wow, would you? Yeah! Just a sec." He rummages in his pack, then pulls out a tablet that looks even older than mine. Grinning ear to ear now, he pulls up a blank screen and hands me a stylus.

"What's your name?"

"Jareth."

Smiling to myself, I write, "To Jareth, a cool kid. Nice meeting you! -Kira Morain #19."

"Awesome," he breathes, reading it. "Thanks! Again!"

"You're welcome. Can you get home all right?"

His head bobs up and down. "Sure, no prob—in fact, that's my zipper now. See ya!" With a last, adoring grin, he sprints for his platform.

I head for my own, still smiling—until I notice *my* zipper just left and the next one's not for twenty-five minutes. "*Flach*," I mutter, glad Mum can't hear me. With a sigh, I pull my own tablet out of my pack. Might as well get a start on tonight's homework while I wait.

When I finally reach Hollydoon's *tapacarr* station, I have to walk nearly a mile to our house, since our supposedly amazing new Sovereign still hasn't gotten around to turning on the antigrav grids outside the village center. Faxon turned them off a few years back to make it easier to monitor people's movements, sidelining the little local zips and rendering my old hovercycle useless.

Now, with the Sovereign's calls to conserve power, I wonder if that'll ever change. I cut through the village center at a brisk pace, trying to make up for lost time.

"Hey, Kira! Great job tonight!"

I turn to see a family of four waving to me from their front porch. Grinning, I wave back. "Thanks!"

"We watched the game, too," a woman calls out of a window of the house next door. "That last goal was amazing!"

Hollydoon is nearly three-quarters Agricultural *fine* so it's not surprising most of the village follows our matches. Still, it's cool to be cheered by my own neighbors.

"We have a great team this year," I call back as more people start waving from windows and doorways. "Be sure to watch our first playoff game in two weeks!"

There are a few cheers and shouts of, "We will!"

I continue on my way, no longer bummed about being so late. The houses get smaller as I move out of Hollydoon's center toward the narrow track that leads across the fields to our farmhouse.

Low stone walls loom past as I leave the village proper, my path lit only by the thick tapestry of stars overhead. I love walking at night now that it's so much safer. Slowing, I gaze up at the constellations. Holographic, of course, but they supposedly look exactly as they would from the surface of Mars. Fake or not, they're pretty.

By the time I reach our farm I'm hoping there's something left from dinner since I'm already hungry again. My post-game fish and chips were more than two hours ago—and nowhere near as filling as a meal at Sheelah's would have been. My parents are watching something on our little living room vidscreen when I come in.

"Oh, Kira, you're home!" Mum greets me with a smile. "We were just discussing the wonderful news."

Pleased and a little surprised, I grin back. They rarely pay attention to my games but this *was* an important one. "Yeah, it was a great match, got us into the playoffs. I guess you saw it on the feeds?"

Mum gives me that vague look she wears way too often these days. "What? Oh, yes, Adina did mention earlier that your team won. I was so excited about Sovereign Emileia's visit to Hollydoon tomorrow, I'm afraid I barely heard her."

"I understand you scored the winning goal?" Dad gets up and gives me a quick hug. "Well done. We'll have to watch the highlights before bed."

"Um, sure." I turn away, hiding my hurt. The villagers and kids at school treat me like a minor celebrity but my own parents can't even be bothered to watch me live on the feeds. "Is there anything left over from dinner? I'm starving."

"I believe so." Mum's gaze has already drifted back to the vidscreen and some other story about the Sovereign. "Why don't you check the recombinator?"

I go into the kitchen to see what my options are. Looks like it was broccoli and synth salmon for dinner again, not exactly my favorites. Probably means that's what there was most of when

Mum went to the marketplace this morning, meaning it was cheapest. Ags, especially less prominent ones like us, never get first pick but there's usually synth salmon and broccoli left over—which means we have it a lot. I quickly scroll through the recombinator menu to see if anything better is stocked. There's not.

Figuring I might as well grab a shower first, I head back through the living room where Mum has reverted to the previous topic.

"I can hardly wait to see her in person," she's saying to Dad. "Consort Galena, her mother, was always so very kind to me when I worked in the Palace gardens..." She trails off, gazing dreamily into space, like she does whenever anything reminds her of the "good old days" before Faxon. Shaking my head, I enter the bedroom I share with my sister.

Adina looks up from her homework when I come in. "Hey. You're home sooner than I thought you'd be. I figured you guys would be partying for hours."

"We couldn't get the party room at Sheelah's after all—had to settle for fish and chips from the place next door." I shrug, my earlier ebullient mood souring further at the memory. "We'll manage a better celebration if we win our first playoff game, though."

Heading into the bathroom, I strip off my *caidpel* uniform, hang it in the ionic cylinder in the corner, then step in myself. In less than two minutes, the dirt and sweat from the game is gone from both my body and the uniform. Pulling on a faded blue tunic and black pants, I go back to the kitchen, where the rest of the family is now gathered.

"—all of us," Mum is saying cheerfully as my sister fills a glass with milk from the chiller that supplies the recombinator. "Won't that be nice?"

"What will be nice?" I ask, crossing to the recombinator myself.

"For us to go as a family to see the Sovereign tomorrow. I'd love for you and Adina to actually meet her," Mum replies. "Especially as she's just about your age."

I try to hide my involuntary grimace. "Younger than me. By at least six months. Anyway, I can't go. I have practice in Monaru tomorrow."

As a member of one of the top *caidpel* teams in Nuath, I have practice six days a week and I *never* skip, unlike some of the others on my team. The coaches are actually fairly flexible if we let them know about conflicts ahead of time, but I've never told my parents that.

"Can't you leave early?" Dad asks with a glance at Mum. "The Sovereign isn't scheduled to start speaking in the square until six."

"Sorry, I really can't. Now that the Ags have made the play-offs, the coaches will be doubling down on us." Which my parents would *know* if they bothered to follow our schedule.

Clearly disappointed, Mum frowns at me. "There *are* more important things than sports, you know, Kira." Not the first time she's said that.

"Your mother is right." At least Dad sounds apologetic. "It was different last season, when you were doing your part for the Resistance, but now that our goals have been achieved, *caidpel* is simply a game, no matter how obsessed some of our citizens may be with it."

"The way some are obsessed with the new Sovereign?" The words are out before I can stop them. "Anyway, what about the crowds? I'll bet most of Hollydoon will be crammed into the village square tomorrow evening."

At that, Mum presses her lips together stubbornly. "I've been doing much better at the Evening Sing the past few weeks. I'm... I'm sure I'll be fine."

Oh, sure, she'll make the effort for those archaic Group Sings most villages resumed once Faxon was out. Or for her beloved Sovereign. But not for my games.

"You know it'll be the same speech as always," I grumble. "The one we've seen on the feeds at least a dozen times." *Those* my parents always remember to watch. "I don't see much point missing practice to hear the same thing again in person. It's not like she writes her own material anyway."

"Kira!" Mum exclaims. "You don't know that."

I roll my eyes. "Seriously? She's only sixteen—and didn't even know Nuath existed until last year. It's not like she's spent her life training for this, like all the previous Sovereigns did."

Mum shakes her head at me sadly. "I don't understand why you're so antagonistic toward Sovereign Emileia, Kira. Most Nuathans understand that she's exactly what we need after the horrors Faxon put us through. Governor Nels did his best, but he was too indecisive to be an effective leader. I truly believe Emileia will become just that. Already, she's beginning to grow into her new role. I think she's shown a great deal of maturity so far, under very trying circumstances."

A laugh escapes me. "Maturity? Like getting caught on camera making out with her Bodyguard, then letting him into her bedroom on their way to Mars? Oh, yeah, that's *exactly* the mature judgment a Sovereign needs."

Dad shoots a concerned glance Mum's way. "Since her Acclamation she's been working closely with Regent Shim to get a properly elected legislature in place, among other things," he points out to me. "Isn't that one of the things you feel strongly about?"

I barely restrain a snort. "I've heard their promises to open up elections to all the *fines*, but who's going to hold them to that? You watch, we'll still end up with nothing but Royals and Scientists in the legislature. They'll never let somebody from Mining or Agriculture bump a Royal out of the *Eodain*, not without a fight."

A fight I fully intend to be a part of, even if all I can use is words.

"They'll have to," Dad insists. "There are barely enough Royals left in Nuath to fill even the *Riogain* these days."

I've heard that on the feeds, too, but I'm not convinced. "The first general election is still a month away," I remind him. "A lot can change by then. Every week more cowardly Royals are coming back from Earth, where they stayed nice and safe while the rest of us had to—"

At Dad's warning glance I break off. He's been more protective of Mum than ever since she got home from that Mind Healing facility in Pryderi a few weeks ago. Even if he's not as big a fan of the Sovereign as Mum, he always shuts me down when I argue politics for fear I'll upset her.

"I'll admit Sovereign Emileia made a few missteps early on, but she's still young," he says. "Give her time."

Shaking my head in frustration, I turn back to the recombinator and punch up a plate of macaroni and cheese. "At least Shim isn't a Royal. If the Sovereign goes back to Earth like she says she will, maybe he'll do a decent job. Though we'd be better off with someone who's actually *lived* here recently, like Crevan Erc. He was planning to—"

"That's enough, Kira," Dad snaps. My parents have never been fans of Crevan or his Populist Party, but I thought he had the right idea.

Mum looks worriedly from Dad to me. "Why don't you bring your plate into the living room, Kira, and we can watch your game highlights together?"

By now, my earlier triumphant mood has been totally ruined. "I don't need to see the highlights, I was there. Besides, it's just a game, right?"

I hate watching myself on the feeds anyway. My hair always looks more red than auburn on the vid. And though I wear it in a messy knot on top of my head when I play, to keep it out of my eyes, it's not a particularly attractive look. Pulling out a fork, I thunk my plate onto the kitchen table and sit down.

Throwing Dad's words back at him only reminded me how much less rewarding my life is these days, without the Resistance. Another reason I have no intention of missing tomorrow's practice. If Brady knows a way I can still make a difference, I absolutely want to hear it.

Order **The Girl From Mars** *now to keep reading!*

A Note from Brenda Hiatt

I know there are many, many books out there to choose from, so I want to take this opportunity to personally thank you for purchasing and reading *Fractured Jewel*. I wrote this novella largely in response to all the readers who kept demanding more Starstruck books after the end of *Starfall*, the fourth book in the series. As I wrote, more ideas kept simmering. Consider *Fractured Jewel* a "bridge," if you will, between my original Starstruck series and future books in that world.

If you enjoyed *Fractured Jewel* (or any of the Starstruck books), please consider leaving a review wherever you buy or talk about books to let like-minded readers know they might enjoy it, too.

About the Author

Brenda Hiatt is the New York Times bestselling author of twenty-two novels (so far), including traditional Regency romance, time travel romance, historical romance, and humorous mystery. She is as excited about her STARSTRUCK series as she's ever been about any of her books. In addition to writing, Brenda is passionate about embracing life to the fullest, to include scuba diving (she has over 60 dives to her credit), Taekwondo (where she recently achieved her 3rd degree black belt), hiking, traveling, and pursuing new experiences and skills.

For a free Starstruck short story and the earliest news about Brenda Hiatt's books, subscribe to her newsletter at:

brendahiatt.com/subscribe